ONCE UPON A VAMPIRE

TALES FROM THE BLOOD COVEN BOOK 1

MARI MANCUSI

1

*J*onathan turned, his azure eyes softening as they fell upon Maisie. Taking a bold step forward, he lowered his head to hers, kissing her softly on one cheek, then the other. His lips were light, tender—the wisp of a butterfly's wing brushing against soft skin.

She lifted her arms, clasping her hands around his neck, pulling him to her. No longer caring if she came off as needy. Desperate. At this point, she would beg if she had to. She would do anything to be with Jonathan one more time. Even if was to be the last.

She could feel his blood tears splashing onto her cheeks as he pulled her into his arms, lifting her as if she weighed nothing at all. Carrying her to the bed covered in black rose petals.

Their last night. Could this truly be their last night?

He gazed at her for a moment with those eyes—those damn eyes that could see into her very soul! Then shook his head. "How can I leave you, Maisie?" he demanded, his voice cracking on the words. "I can't. I won't!'

"You have no choice," she said sadly.

And they both knew it was true.

I LOOKED up from the book, my gaze raking over my rapt audience. As always, not a dry eye in the house. I set the book down.

"If you want to know the rest, you'll have to buy your own copy," I teased.

The audience laughed, effectively breaking the spell. As they broke out into applause I tried not to squirm in my seat.

"Thank you all for coming," Darla, my assistant, broke in, stepping up behind my table. "Hannah will now sign any copies you have purchased tonight from the store. Then, if there's time left over, she can sign up to three of your older titles. But that's all," She added with a scolding grin. "Our girl needs to get back to writing, after all!"

More applause. People began to line up. I opened my Sharpie, preparing myself for the rest of the evening. We had two hours before the bookstore closed, which wasn't nearly enough time to get through the line, judging from past experiences.

Darla was always telling me to go faster. To churn through readers and not talk to each one of them so long. Maybe skip the whole selfie thing. But how could I possibly do that? They had come all this way. At times driven hours or sat through traffic. They had stood in line. They each deserved at least a moment dedicated to them alone.

Some bookstores—especially the indie ones--would keep their doors open longer, to allow me to at least get through the initial line. But now, with thirteen titles in the *Jonathan and Maisie Vampire Chronicles*, there was no way I could sign them all.

It was a good problem to have, of course. An author's dream come true to have readers so dedicated they'd cart your books into the store in a rolly bag, hoping to get every last one of them signed. I just wished it didn't exacerbate my carpal tunnel so much. Or fray on my already pathetic nerves.

And so I forced Darla to play bad cop. A job which she took

on with relish. I, on the other hand, would probably sign until my fingers fell off rather than turn anyone away. Especially those who showed up in costumes. Tonight I had spotted a few amazing Maisies in the crowd, dressed in her signature neck-plunging crimson gown from the first book in the series, *Blood and Roses*.

All the better to bite you, my dear! (One of Jonathan's first iconic lines.)

Speaking of Jonathan... My eyes rose to the back of the room. To the man who had stepped in while I'd been reading, causing me to nearly stop mid-sentence. I squinted at him now, trying to get a better look. He was dressed all in black, rocking an old-fashioned regency era suit paired with a dashing white cravat. The kind of outfit Maisie was always trying to get Jonathan to throw away. (Okay, fine, she secretly thought he looked pretty hot in it, it just didn't work for your typical taco Tuesday. My vampire hero may have loved his iPhone, but he'd never warm up to hipster chic.)

Even from here I could tell the guy's outfit looked authentic. Definitely not a costume in a bag via Party City. I needed to examine him closer when he reached the front of the line. I was always looking for good Jonathan costumes as we often brought an actor to events to roleplay my hero with fans. (Something they adored!)

I shook my head. There would be time for costume appreciation later. Right now it was time for me to get to work. And so I started to sign, writing an inspirational message in each and every book, closing with a vampire smiley face and the phrase, "Fangs and Kisses!" before the actual autograph. It was admittedly a lot to write in each book and I knew Darla was giving me the evil eye, but I ignored her, instead inviting the fan to take a selfie with me before I moved on to the next reader.

The bookstore manager had informed us earlier they'd

presold 300 books for the event and that was just the new release. Which was crazy! It never ceased to amaze me how many people had devoted their lives—and wallets—to this world created by little 23-year-old me.

When I first started writing *Blood and Roses*, I hadn't even been able to find a publisher for it. Everyone claimed vampire books were "dead" after the whole *Twilight* boom and bust. And no editor would touch my little paranormal romance with a ten-foot stake. So I'd decided to self-publish it, putting it up online, figuring at least this way family and friends would be able to buy it and read it.

I honestly expected to sell ten copies. Instead, I sold half a million in the first year. Suddenly agents were knocking at my door. Publishers drooling on my pages. Everyone wanted a piece of Maisie and Jonathan.

And more books. Always more books.

It had started out exhilarating. Not to mention flattering. But lately it had become a bit exhausting, too, not that I'd ever admit it to my readers. I'd had to drop out of college to keep up with my deadlines and I'd hired Darla, my best friend, to become my official assistant. Darla kept track of my appearances, updated my Facebook and Twitter, and made sure I always had groceries in my fridge when I was on deadline. (And I was always on deadline.)

It did make me feel a bit guilty from time to time—especially the day I caught her cleaning my very neglected toilet. But I made up for it by offering her a healthy six figure salary, which allowed her to quit her hated day job as an executive assistant at a grumpy tax assessor's office.

"Oh my God! I am SO in LOVE with Jonathan!" swooned a college aged girl with black hair and a nose-ring as she stepped up to my table to get her book signed. "My Mom gave me the first book last year and I totally thought it was going to be lame, you know? Most of the stuff she reads is such trash. But *your* book! Oh. My. God. It spoke to me!" She paused, then added, her eyes shining, "It was like I WAS Maisie."

I smiled and thanked her and signed her book. It was crazy that even after all this time I still got so flummoxed when fans gushed about my work. I mean, I may have been an international bestselling author but at the end of the day I was still only me—the most introverted girl in the known universe. If I had a choice, I would never leave my house. Hell, I'd hire a body double to do these events.

But my new publisher was having none of that. Publicity and public appearances were all part of the game, they said. And it was important to get face time with one's fans. (Real face time, as opposed to FaceTime, which could have been done from home.) And so every time a new book came out, I got my hair blown out, my eyebrows waxed, my makeup refreshed. Then I'd head out on tour for three to four exhausting, mind-numbing weeks.

From time to time I would try to argue my case with my publisher—that they would get far more books from me if I could just skip the touring part of the job. But they only laughed and sent me more plane tickets.

"Thank you *so* much!" the girl squealed, hugging the newly signed book to her chest. She turned to leave, then stopped in her tracks. "Oh!" she cried. "I almost forgot!"

I watched, curious, as she reached into her bag, pulling out a string of dark purple rosary beads. Just like the ones Maisie kept in her sock drawer. She set it down on the table.

"My mom wanted you to have this," she said. "Just in case you ever run into a *real* vampire."

I raised an eyebrow. "Real vampire?" I repeated.

The girl laughed. "I know, I know," she said. "But just take it, okay? It'll make my mom's day."

I smiled. "Tell her thank you," I said, reaching for the necklace. Then I handed it to Darla. "Put it in my purse, okay?" I said. "So I don't leave it here by mistake."

Darla did as I asked and the girl danced away happily. I sighed, suddenly feeling very weary. When Darla returned, she gave me a concerned once over.

"Are you okay, Hannah?" she asked. "Do you need another Red Bull?"

"I'm okay, thanks," I assured her. The last thing I needed was more caffeine to jangle my already fraught nerves. "But another Sharpie wouldn't go amiss." I shook the marker I was using. "This one's on its last leg."

"Seriously, I should have taken out stock in Sharpie before you hit the bestseller list," Darla snorted. But she scurried away to find the store manager and get me a new pen.

And so I signed. And I signed. Then I took a photo and signed some more. It seemed like forever before the line started to dwindle and the store began to go through the motions of shutting down. Your total normal book signing, really, except for one thing. The guy in the Jonathan costume, hovering in the back of the store, but never getting into line for an autograph like everyone else.

Was he not here to see me after all? But no, that costume was a dead giveaway. Maybe his wife made him wear it—I did see couples' costumes from time to time. But there was no one in line left who was dressed like Maisie.

Maybe he was just shy. I definitely could relate to that. Still, he was creeping me out a little, hovering at the back, watching me as I worked the line.

Finally, I made it to the end. A young girl, probably about my age danced up to the table. She was wearing a *Vampires R People Too* t-shirt and had blue streaks in her blond hair. She thrust her well-worn book in my direction.

"Hi!" she said, giggling with nervous excitement. "Can you, like, sign my book?"

"Of course!" I said, smiling back at her. "Especially since you waited so long. And I love that you have one of the original self-published covers of *Blood and Roses*. There aren't too many of those around anymore."

"I know, right?" she practically squealed. "And I have to say, it's way better than the publisher one, no offense. I mean, the cuts they made you do when they republished it?" She shook her head. "So not cool."

I shrugged. "Editors," I said, as if that explained everything.

"Yeah. Well, the problem is I keep re-reading this one. And it's getting way worn out." She sighed. "I'd buy a new one but these are going for like five hundred bucks on eBay."

"You know, I think I have a stack of the old covers at home," I told her. "Here's my assistant's card. Email her your address and tell her you talked to me and she'll send you one."

The girls' blue eyes widened into saucers. "Oh my God! Thank you! Are you sure? I mean, I could pay you! Er, not what they charge on eBay but, you know."

I waved her off. "They're just sitting in the closet, collecting dust. I'd much rather have Jonathan and Maisie go to a good home and be well-loved."

"Oh I will love Jonathan, all right!" the girl joked, practically swooning as she put her hand to her heart. "He is SUCH the perfect man. So gentle and sweet and passionate." She gave me a knowing look. "Some vampire authors? They don't get it right. You obvious know how to write *real* vampires."

"Are you fucking kidding me?"

I looked up, surprised to hear the deep baritone voice interrupt her rambling. My eyes widened as they fell upon none other than the guy who had been hovering in the back of the store since the beginning of the signing. I hadn't even seen him move, but suddenly he was there, standing right in front of my table. Looking down at my books, his upper lip curled into what appeared to be an actual sneer.

The girl also leapt at the voice, whirling around. She clearly hadn't heard him either. She stared at him for a moment, then practically jumped up and down in delight.

"Oh my God! You got someone to play Jonathan!" she cried, her excitement making her voice squeaky. "That is so cool. God, he looks great, too. I mean, I've seen some of the Jonathans you've gotten for other events—the DragonCon parade, Comic Con, the RT Convention. But this guy. He is per-fec-tion."

I had to agree. In fact, I couldn't stop looking at him. He was so tall. So broad shouldered. His cheekbones looked as if they'd been cut of glass, complimenting his angular jaw. His mouth was thin and almost cruel looking. And his eyes—sweet baby Jesus! —those eyes! Piercing diamonds with just a hint of cerulean circling deep black pupils.

(Yes, that's quite the description, I know. But hey, I'm a romance writer. It's what I do.)

I realized the girl was waiting for me to say something. "Actually," I said. "I didn't hire him. I think he's a...reader?"

Even as I made this suggestion I couldn't believe it to be true. My readers were awesome. But this guy somehow didn't seem the type.

Sure enough, his sneer dipped to a critical frown. 'Um, no," he said curtly. "I am *not* a reader."

"Oh! But you should be!" the girl cried, totally undeterred. I blushed, wanting to beg her to stop. I needed this guy to go away —just having him standing there was making my nerves taut as piano wire.

But the girl pushed on. As my fans always did. They were worse than drug dealers when it came to trying to hook people on my series. "These books are amazing!" she cried, waving one of them in his face. "The way Miss Miller describes Jonathan...-"

"Yes. I heard her...*description*."

"Then you know!" she squealed, clearly not catching the sarcasm in his tone. "I mean, I've read a lot of vampire books. But none of them compare to Miss Miller's. She's...amazing. It's like she knows vampires."

A shadow seemed to cross over the man's face. For a moment he said nothing. Then, "Have you ever met an actual vampire?" he asked quietly.

The girl blushed bright red. "Well, no. Of course not. But—"

"Then how do you know her characters are realistic?"

The fan glanced helplessly at me. "Well, you know. I mean..."

"In fact, I'd be willing to bet Miss Miller doesn't know *anything* about real vampires. Or," he added, leveling that intense gaze on me. His eyes so piercing they made me shiver. "Real *men* for that matter." He paused, then added, "And evidently neither do her readers."

Oh my God. I stared at the guy, so shocked and taken aback that for a moment I couldn't find words. I mean, I'd known he wasn't a fan. But I never would have pinned him as an outright troll.

"You're out of line," I said, rising to my feet. "You don't know anything about me or my readers."

His lip curled. "Don't I?" he asked. "You cash in on titillating, female-driven fantasies about vampires who don't act like vampires. Not to mention men who do not act like men." He paused, then added, "How am I doing so far?"

"I don't think that's--"

"Let me give you a word of advice," he interrupted. "Real men don't make love with the gentleness of a butterfly's wing. Real men--"

"And I think we're done here." Darla broke in, grabbing the book out of my hand and handing it back to the blue-haired girl, who had finally been rendered speechless. I watched as she backed away from my table, then practically ran to the door.

"You forgot my card!" I called out after her. But she was already gone. Leaving Darla and me alone in the darkened bookstore with Mr. So Not Jonathan.

His blazing eyes locked on me. Fierce, challenging. It was all I could do not to turn away. Instead, I squared my shoulders, meeting those dark eyes with my own. As if daring him to continue. Though truth be told I wasn't exactly sure if my insides could take him elaborating on his earlier point.

And, of course, Darla was having none of it. She stepped in between us, hands on her hips. "The bookstore is closed and Miss Miller is leaving," she informed him in no uncertain terms. "So unless you'd like a book signed, I suggest you take that attitude and get the hell out of here." Her implied look screamed: *unless you want to deal with me.*

His lip curled again. He grabbed a book from the pile and tossed it in front of me. Awesome.

"By all means," he said with a smug smile. "Please sign my book."

I almost flat out refused. My hands were shaking like mad and my heart was close to panic attack level. Which was ridiculous, of course. After all, like any author, I'd had more than my share of trolls. I was used to dealing with haters.

But this guy—he just had this presence. Like he filled the room just by standing in it. You could look away, but your gaze would always return to him. To his piercing eyes. To his black hair, shiny, even under the dim bookstore lights. And the way he moved! Graceful as a feline, yet exuding masculinity at the same time. As if there was something deeper, more powerful, rippling in the air around him. Causing a desire to radiate inside of me that felt almost feral in its intensity.

And...this is why you don't date, I scolded myself.

I cleared my throat. 'You don't have to buy a book," I told him. "I mean, I don't care. And honestly it sounds like it might not be your cup of tea."

"I'll be the one to make that decision, thank you," he said, thrusting the book in my direction again.

"Fine. It's your money. Who should I make it out to?"

"Logan. Logan Valcourt."

"Sounds like a vampire name," I said with a small laugh, desperate to lighten the mood.

He didn't smile. Of course. Instead, he just stood there, waiting patiently for me to sign. I grabbed my Sharpie and turned to the title page. Addressing the book to him and managing to sign my name, even with my hand shaking. I left off the "Fangs and Kisses" part. It seemed too pat—too cute for his tastes.

When I was finished, I handed him the book. "Thank you," he said, as if amused. "I appreciate you taking the time."

And with that, he vacated the bookstore. So quickly it seemed like at one moment he was there and the next he was simply gone. I turned to Darla trying to calm my nerves.

"So...that was weird."

She snorted. "Weird doesn't even begin to cover that."

"What was he doing here? Why did he buy a book if he hated my character?"

"Maybe he wanted to give you a shitty review on his blog. Who knows?" Darla shrugged. "Whatever. Shake it off, Hannah. He's gone."

"Yeah," I said, grabbing my favorite pen. "He was something though, don't you think? I mean, he had this presence."

"Don't think I didn't notice!" Darla pretended to fan herself. "After all, tall, dark and Asshole is totally my jam."

I laughed. "Too bad he's such a jerk. I would totally hire him to play Jonathan."

"I have a feeling he'd turn down that particular honor."

"Yeah," I agreed, staring absently at the back of the now empty store, where the guy had been hovering all night. It was so strange. He'd stayed for the entire reading, then waited until the very last person in line stepped up before making his move.

"Real vampires don't make love," Darla mimicked with a laugh. "Man, where did he get *that* line? You need to use that in a book someday!"

I shook my head, grabbing my stuff off the table. "He'd probably sue me," I said, my mind flashing back to him standing there again and my heart giving a weird pang in my chest.

He was an asshole, I reminded myself. *A good looking asshole, but that's all. And after tonight you'll never see him again.*

2

My cat, Spike, mewed in greeting as I pushed open my front door and stepped inside my apartment. He wrapped himself around my legs, almost tripping me as I fumbled for the light switch. It was our daily routine; he pretended he was happy to see me and I kept him well-stocked in kitty litter and catnip.

I reached down, patting him on the head. He took the public display of affection for exactly three seconds, then darted over to his food bowl, looking up at me with accusing eyes. I should have gotten a dog. They weren't so judgmental.

"I know, I know," I said, reaching into the cupboard to grab the cat food. "I'm late. There were a lot of people there. I couldn't just turn them away."

Spike seemed to roll his eyes at this. He had no issues with turning people away. In fact, turning people away was his typical MO. I was the only one he allowed to touch him and then only sporadically when he was in the mood. Otherwise we both kept to ourselves, the consummate roommates.

"You should be happy," I scolded him. "Darla wanted me to go out for drinks. I could have been hours later."

Spike swished his tail, his eyes not leaving the bag of food. I sighed. He knew better than anyone that I would never have taken Darla up on her offer. She knew it, too, when she'd offered. But she always did, anyway. As if she felt guilty going out and having a good time while I returned to my empty (sorry Spike) apartment alone.

But I didn't begrudge her a good time. And I wished she wouldn't begrudge me my solitude. She couldn't understand how I could live in a tiny apartment with towering bookshelves on almost every available surface. She'd told me a thousand times I should move—I had the money now—I could get a real house. With a real library and a master suite with a Jacuzzi tub and walk-in shower.

But while the library part sounded cool, I wasn't interested in a house I could get lost in. This place was mine. Cozy, cramped, but comfortable. I felt safe here. Spike and I had our routine down and there were no surprises. Nothing to bring on the anxiety. It was my haven, my retreat when things in the outside world got to be too much. When the signing lines were long or the fans were rowdy, I could picture this place. My well-worn sofa, my Apple TV. My faithful computer in the corner, surrounded by vampire tchotchkes that fans had sent me over the years. It all dampened the screaming anxiety to a dull roar.

No granite countertop or six burner range in the world could make up for that luxury.

I sat down on the couch in question now, fidgeting a little, still wired from the event. I hated that feeling—being tired, but unable to sleep. On nights like this, if I didn't do my trick, I would be up for hours, staring at the wall, actively trying to keep the panic at bay as I thought back to all the people. Surrounded by people.

I leaned back on the couch. *They were all friends,* I told myself, going through my routine. *They all loved you. They loved your books. They only wanted to meet you.* The flashes from their smart phones burned against my irises. *They wanted to post your picture on Facebook to brag to their friends. They're part of your family. They love Jonathan, they love Maisie. They love you.*

Except the guy who hadn't.

My gut clenched as my mind flashed back to the tall, dark stranger at the back of the room again. Logan Valcourt. Hot asshole extraordinaire. Why had he come? What did he want? His eyes seemed to burn into me, even now. Cutting and cruel and angry. Why had he bought a book? Why had he said those things about me?

Not that they weren't true. At the end of the day, he was right. What I wrote about vampires? Just a mash-up of what I'd seen on TV and read in other books. I hadn't done any real research into the entire mythos—just sampled popular culture and made up the rest. It usually made Darla and I giggle when people would write online about how my vampires were "realistic" unlike other authors'. How could something made up be real?

And as for the not knowing men, well, that was more than a given. I hadn't had a boyfriend since *before*. And I doubted I would ever have one again. But that suited me just fine. After all, I had a busy, successful life. I had dozens of well-loved book boyfriends. And I had Jonathan. Jonathan, the perfect man. The perfect vampire. The one who could always guarantee me a happily ever after.

Real life was just too risky.

I walked over to the keyboard and smiled. "Hey Jonathan," I whispered, feeling a little silly doing it. I sank down into my computer chair and loaded up my latest work in progress. *Dreams with the Vampire* would be the fourteenth novel in the series and I was determined to make it the best.

I began to type.

"*JONATHAN ARE YOU OKAY?*"

Maisie looked up to see the vampire stalk into the room. She frowned.

"*What's wrong?*" *she asked, taking a worried step backward. She'd never seen him like this. His eyes were cutting, cruel. Angry.*

He grabbed her and shoved her against the wall. His lips pressing against hers, cruel and punishing. She opened her mouth to protest and his tongue dove in.

"*You think you know everything, don't you?*" *he snarled as he came up for air.* "*But you know nothing at all.*"

I LEANED BACK in my chair, frowning. Where had *that* come from? Jonathan did not accost Maisie. They were in love. They respected one another. She was safe from him. He never scared her.

He wasn't like *him*.

I shuddered as the all too familiar fear trickled down my back, causing my pulse to rise and my heart to beat faster in my chest. I rose from my seat, checking the windows, checking the doors. That was another nice thing about having a small place, though I wouldn't have admitted this to anyone. But it was easy to keep on top of. I checked the windows again, then the door. But my pulse still raced.

And so I walked over to the bookcase. I grabbed the box. The beautiful handcrafted wooden vampire puzzle box, made from wood harvested from the Carpathian Mountains. It had been stained turquoise blue on the outside and lined in the richest velvet on the inside. I ran my hand across the top of it, taking a deep breath. Just seeing the box gave me back a small bit of control. Sometimes that was all I needed.

But not tonight. Tonight with the huge crowd, with the man who looked like Jonathan but wasn't. Tonight I needed something more. And so I opened the box and I pulled out the razor blade. It gleamed in the candlelight of my apartment and I sucked in a breath. Then I put it to my arm, closing my eyes. Letting all my worries flee my mind as I concentrated on dragging the blade down the inside of my arm. Watching the small trail of crimson appear behind it.

It was beautiful.

And I was at peace once again.

3

"So who is this guy again?" I asked grumpily as Darla worked on my hair. It was hopeless as usual, of course. My crazy corkscrew curls kept escaping her attempted up-do, no matter how much gel she used.

"You tell me," she said with a shrug. "All the invitation said was that the gala was being held in your honor and that the proceeds would support your favorite charity."

"Which is the only reason I'm agreeing to any of this," I huffed, yanking down at the sleeves of my gown, feeling itchy and uncomfortable in my dress. Whoever this anonymous bene-factor was, he certainly didn't know me well if he expected me to delight in the spotlight of this kind of thing.

In fact, it was pretty much the anti-me. Dressing up, hobnob-bing with rich people who likely saw my books as nothing more than poorly written mommy porn. I mean, to each his own—I didn't begrudge them their opinions. But that didn't mean I had to spend quality time with them, defending my books.

But in the end, it was an offer I couldn't refuse. Not when the invitation promised a minimum of thirty-thousand dollars going to RAINN, my favorite charity group. And so I sucked it up and donned a dress and tried to mentally prepare myself for the required mingling and small talk.

In other words I was pre-drinking like a boss.

"Are you sure you want to wear that?" Darla asked, giving the dress in question a critical once-over. "It's like ninety degrees out today. It may be boiling in the ballroom."

"I'll be fine," I assured her.

She narrowed her eyes at me. "You haven't been...you know...have you?"

"No!" I cried making my voice as indignant as I could. "You know I don't do that anymore."

"Okay, okay!" She held up her hands. "I was just checking."

"I just don't want people to see the old scars," I lied. "That's all."

But, of course, that wasn't all. In fact, I'd been pulling out my Carpathian puzzle box every night this week. I didn't know why, exactly. Just that ever since that night at the bookstore my nerves had been fraying at the ends. To the point where it was actually starting to interfere with my daily writing word count. And I so didn't have time for *anything* to interfere with my writing. Not when my book was due in three weeks and I wasn't even half done with it.

Which also meant I didn't have time for shit like this. An evening at a gala meant an evening not writing. And when I did finally meet my so-called benefactor tonight, I would have a thing or two to say to him, charity or no.

"You sure you don't want me to come?" Darla asked, giving me a worried look.

For a split second I contemplated saying yes. That I needed her there—that I couldn't do this without her. But in the end, I shook my head. I knew she had scored tickets to the Imagine Dragons concert tonight and had been eagerly anticipating the show for months. She didn't deserve to miss out on something so epic just to babysit little old me. I was a big girl. I needed to do this myself.

"I'm sure," I said. "You go to the concert. Have fun."

She pursed her lips. "And you'll be okay?"

"I'll be fine. I mean, it's just a party, right? What could possibly go wrong?"

THE GALA WAS BEING HELD in a beautiful old mansion on the far side of town. The type you'd expect to see in some Great Gatsby movie remake with expansive lawns and overly manicured shrubbery. It was already packed by the time I arrived and the valet was working overtime, moving cars that probably cost more than the GNP of several small countries. Whoever this guy was, he clearly knew all the right people.

I was definitely not one of these people.

My driver walked around the car, opening my door and putting out his hand to help me step out. I took it, trying not to wobble on my ridiculously high heels. Darla had not only forced me to wear heels, she had dragged me to Nordstrom's earlier that afternoon to buy a decent pair. Something I didn't appreciate at the time, but now realized, judging from the other guests, was the right move. If I didn't sprain an ankle, that was.

Once on my feet, I thanked the driver. He told me to text him when I was ready to go home. I agreed, then turned to the house, sucking in a breath, trying to still my fast-beating heart.

You can do this, I told myself. *It's for a good cause. The best cause.*

I started up the front steps, feeling heat prickle under my arms in the warm night. My dress, which had already felt hot in my air-conditioned home was now scorching my skin and sweat was already dripping between my breasts.

But there was no turning back now. And so I pushed onward, walking past the line of people posing for photos in front of the mansion. Praying the place would have proper AC.

I needn't have worried. The inside of the mansion was even more opulent than the outside and thankfully properly chilled. In addition, every corner seemed to be carved in marble and trimmed in gold. Fancy chandeliers dripped diamonds of light from the beautiful fresco ceiling, the intricately painted cherubs frolicking with rapturous mortals.

What was I doing here? This was *so* not my world. Sure, I made a lot of money selling books, but that was probably spare change in the couch cushions to the other people here. I looked around, desperate to locate a familiar face—would I know *anyone* here? Someone from the charity foundation we were raising money for perhaps? Another author? Maybe a caterer I had gone to college with? But no, I didn't I recognize a soul in this sea of well-dressed strangers.

This was going to be a very long night.

Finally, I made my way over to the bar. Always a safe haven in a storm. I slipped onto a stool and ordered a glass of champagne. When in Rome, right? A few moments later the bartender returned, placing the glass in front of me. I picked it up, pulling it to my lips, almost choking on the bubbles as I attempted to drink too quickly. Desperate to soothe my frazzled nerves.

"May I have this dance?"

I whirled around, startled by the sudden voice. My eyes widened in surprise as they fell upon broad shoulders, dark hair, pale skin and oddly piercing blue eyes.

Vampire, my brain niggled before I could help myself.

I know this sounds crazy, but for a split second, I truly thought it was Jonathan, my vampire hero, sprung off the page of one of my books and standing before me in real life, asking me, of all people, to dance with him.

But, of course, it wasn't. And a moment later I realized exactly who it actually was, standing before me.

Logan Valcourt. The stranger from my book signing.

I hadn't realized how much I'd been still thinking about that whole thing until my eyes raked over him now. But suddenly I realized he hadn't left my brain since that night at the bookstore. Not entirely anyway. The encounter had been lurking in the shadows of my memories all this time, waiting patiently to reemerge.

Just as he, himself, evidently.

Because now he was here. Inexplicably standing in front of me. A shiver ran down my spine—and not one entirely made up of fear.

"You!" I cried, almost falling off my barstool and spilling my drink. "What are you doing here?" Seriously in all the galas in all the world. He had to walk into mine?

A smile played at the corner of his mouth. "It's nice to see you again, too, Hannah Miller."

I nodded dumbly, not sure how to respond. The way his mouth moved was weirdly mesmerizing and I was a bit concerned I might actually be drooling as I stared at him, dumb-founded. And who could blame me, really? I mean, my God, he was good looking. His dark hair slicked back tonight, offering up a better look at his intense blue eyes which were framed by black lashes so thick you could imagine he was wearing guyliner. His nose was strong, as was his jaw. And his lips were full and generous. And as for his body? Even hidden under his tuxedo, you could tell it was magnificent. Like one of those Greek statues I'd seen in the ballroom. I had to fight the urge not to run my hands down his chest to see if it was actually made of marble.

Thankfully I managed to restrain myself from that ridiculous notion and I realized he was waiting for me to say something. You know, like in a normal conversation between two people where they both talked and one didn't stare at the other like a slobbering mess. I cleared my throat.

"Well, thank you for coming," I managed to squeak. "It's a very worthy cause."

"Indeed," he said, letting the word hang there for a moment, as if it were a gourmet dessert to be savored before swallowed. Then he added, "But you haven't answered my question."

For a moment I stared at him dumbly, trying to rack my brain. Had he asked me a question? Then suddenly his opening line came raging back to me and I felt my cheeks flush.

"I don't dance," I said.

He gave me a skeptical look. "You don't *like* to dance?" he asked. "Or you don't know *how* to dance?"

"Um..." My brain raced, trying to decide which option would best dissuade further follow-up. Or, you know, an actual dance. "I really don't know how."

His smile widened and I realized I should have picked door number one. "There's nothing to it," he assured me. "Just let me lead." He put out a hand, giving me an expectant look.

I stared down at his hand. I didn't want to take it. At the same time, I wanted to take it so badly it hurt. What was wrong with me? Finally, I gave in, slipping my hand into his own, which was so large it practically swallowed mine up entirely. Electricity sparked instantly, as if we really were in a romance novel and I almost knocked over my champagne for the second time. (For the record, I would have made a very lousy romance heroine.) Instead, I tipped it back, taking a large slug and draining it dry. (Classy, right?) Then I allowed myself to be led to my doom...or, you know, the dance floor. Same thing, really.

He pulled me into his arms with a determination that startled me, his hand secured at the small of my back, the other sliding into my own. I let him do it, barely able to breathe as I dared to look up into his eyes again. He looked dark, dangerous. Sexy as hell, too, if we were being honest here. And yet there was a slight amusement dancing across his face as well.

I frowned at this. He clearly thought I was out of my league. And while he wasn't wrong, of course, I wasn't about to let him take pleasure in my discomfort. And so I drew in a breath and tried to recall all those ballroom dance lessons my mom had forced on me as a kid. Maybe they hadn't been good for nothing after all.

The steps came back quicker than I had hoped and soon I was keeping up with him, gliding across the dance floor with a grace that surprised even me. I met his eyes, my expression bordering on defiance. As if to say, who's laughing now?

"And here I thought you couldn't dance," he remarked in a low voice. "Turns out you're a regular Ginger Rogers."

I shrugged, hoping I wasn't noticeably blushing under the dance floor lights. "Thanks," I said. "It's been a while. But I guess it's like riding a bike."

"I wouldn't know," he said. "I've never ridden a bike."

The music swelled then and he spun me around, then pulled me back into his arms. His hand burned at my lower back, causing my stomach to flip flop like a fish out of water. It'd been so long since I'd been in a man's arms, I'd forgotten what it felt like. And while I knew in my heart I should pull away, put distance between us, it was as if my body had transformed into nothing but iron shavings while he had become an industrial strength magnet, drawing me back to him every time I managed to squeeze an inch apart.

I cleared my throat. I had to break this spell somehow. This wasn't me. I didn't do dances with strangers. Even if they did have an uncanny resemblance to my vampire hero.

"What are you doing here, anyway?" I found myself blurting out.

His lip curled. "Hosting a benefit to your favorite charity, of course."

I stopped in my tracks. Stared at him in disbelief. "What?" I squeaked. "This is *your* benefit?"

He shrugged. "Did I not tell you?"

"No. You did not tell me. Of course you didn't tell me!"

"Then why did you come?"

A blush rose to my cheeks. "It was for charity."

"I see," he said, nodding. "But this is not your scene." It wasn't a question.

I snorted. "This is about as far from my *scene* as you can possibly get and still be a scene at all. I don't like public places. I don't like people."

He raised an eyebrow. "What about adoring fans?"

"That's different," I insisted, angry that I'd let him put me on the defensive. "That's for work. Not for fun."

"And what do you do for fun?"

Now my face was on fire. I knew if I told him the truth, he would laugh at me. Think me pathetic and small—well, more than he probably already did.

"Hang gliding," I said, blurting out the first thing that came to my head. Which was actually pretty odd, since I'd never in my life gone hang gliding.

He laughed, a low rich laugh that danced like music across my ears, despite my best efforts. "You *hang glide?*" he repeated. "Now that *is* unexpected."

"Yeah, well, maybe you don't have me all figured out after all."

Anger burned in me now. Anger at him for laughing at me. At myself for falling for any of this. It was all a set-up, I realized suddenly. The whole event, orchestrated by this rich asshole to get me here. Would my charity even receive the money it was promised? Or was that just another ruse?

"I know all I need to know," he replied smoothly. "After all, I read your book."

Wait what?

"You actually read it?" I demanded, despite myself. So much for playing it cool.

"Yes."

"Did you...like it?"

"Not particularly."

I groaned. Of course.

"Then why are you doing all this? Why would you hold a big crazy charity event for an author you don't even like?"

"I didn't say I didn't like the *author*."

I pulled myself out of his grasp. "Sorry buddy. It doesn't work like that. You can't insult my book without insulting me."

This wasn't remotely true, of course. In fact, I had pretty much made it my life mission not to read reviews or deal with haters. I knew full well once I put my art out into the world I was giving up control over how people consumed it. Those who trashed me online might be having just as much fun hating on my books as those who loved and adored them. And who was I to dictate how my work should be consumed by strangers?

Or as Darla put it: don't feed the trolls.

But that was online. A web browser I could click closed at a moment's notice. A computer I could turn off and walk away from. Even at book signings if we had a heckler show up we could have security whisk him away. But now, here I was at this fancy ball, supposedly thrown in my honor to support my favorite charity, by a man who hated my work and wasn't afraid to tell me so to my face.

"Excuse me," I managed to say. "I've actually got to...Yeah."

I broke free of his grasp, which was surprisingly strong,

bolting across the room in search of an exit, my heart pounding in my chest as the walls seemed to close in around me. It was suddenly all too much, too weird, and I needed to get some air. Maybe it was stupid not to bring Darla with me—or have some other chaperone. I thought I could handle myself alone. But now…

My arm itched. As I ran, pushing past people, I found myself reaching down to yank up my sleeve. Just a tiny bit—so as not to be noticed, my thumbnail scratching against the inside of my wrist. Trying desperately to calm myself down the one way I knew I could. If I could just get somewhere alone I could dig out the blade I had buried in my purse. Give myself some real relief.

Finally, I managed to locate an exit and I burst out the door into the warm night air, sucking in a much needed breath. Thankfully it was quiet out here, most people were now inside. I looked around at the beautiful manicured gardens, trying to steady my pulse. I had to admit, the place was beautiful. Expertly lit so you could still see the stars above proudly showing off a celestial portrait spread across the night sky.

I reached into my purse, digging deep. Looking for—

"Hannah!"

I looked up with a groan. Of course. I should have known there was no way Mr. Tall, Dark and Asshole would have just let me make an easy escape. I took my hand out of my purse, my heart stuttering in my chest. Now, standing alone, away from the crowd, I felt stupid for my earlier reaction. All he did was say he didn't like my book. And I, like a child, had literally run away from this perceived rejection.

Pathetic, Hannah. Truly pathetic.

"Sorry," I mumbled as he approached, looking, to his credit, legitimately concerned. "I just…needed some air."

"No." He shook his head. "I'm the one who's sorry. I didn't mean to anger you. I just wanted to be honest."

"Well, mission accomplished. Now leave me alone."

"Don't you want to know why I didn't like the book?"

"Actually I couldn't care less."

"I don't believe that for a second," he said. "Otherwise you wouldn't have been so angry in there."

"Uh, maybe I just don't appreciate being told my book sucks?"

"I didn't say it sucked. I said I didn't care for it."

I closed my eyes frustration washing over me. "Fine. You didn't *care* for it. Couldn't you have just left a GoodReads review like everyone else? Or sent my publisher a scathing letter? Why the whole crazy party ruse?"

"Because I wanted to get to know you better," he said simply.

My eyes flew open, realizing he was now standing in front of me. Standing too close, invading my space. I tried to stumble backward, but I hit the trunk of a tree. He smiled at this, looking smug, the cat that ate the canary. Then he stepped closer still, his thigh brushing up against my own, sending crazy chills all the way to my extremities.

"Don't come any closer," I managed to scrape out. "I'll scream."

He complied immediately, stepping back, bowing his head respectfully. Which should have made me feel relieved. Instead, I felt a weird shimmer of disappointment fluttering inside me. As if his unexpected advance had fired something up in me, only to be snuffed out again. Which sounded insane, but was par for the course tonight.

He reached out and my breath caught in my throat as he swept an errant curl from my face. His eyes had softened now and the smug smile had vanished. In fact, if I didn't know better I'd say he almost looked...sad.

"I'm sorry," he said. "I forget myself. Please. Allow me to escort you back to the party."

"No," I said, hating how flushed my face felt. "I think I'll stay out here."

His mouth dipped to a frown. "Do you not like the party?"

"It's a great party," I admitted. "Just...I don't really do parties. Even great ones."

He laughed. "Perhaps next time I should arrange for us to go *hang gliding* instead."

I groaned. "There's really no need. Seriously, next time you get the urge to hate on my books, just go online like everyone else. Or hold a book burning—that could be fun." I snorted. "Or better yet, don't read any more of them. They're clearly not to your taste."

His eyes settled on me, dark and piercing. As if he were reaching out, stroking me with deft fingers, even though in reality he remained a respectful distance away.

"What?" I demanded.

"I have a question."

I sighed. "What?"

"How do you...research your books?"

"They're about vampires, dude. I make shit up."

He looked incredulous. "Off the top of your head?"

"And the bottom of my dark, dark twisted soul. Yes."

"No wonder you get them wrong," he muttered.

"God, are we back on this? Look, dude, you may be pretty, but you're clearly deluded. Let me set you straight. The books I write? They ain't memoirs. They're fantasy. Those vampires I talk about? They're not real. Because vampires don't exist."

My voice rose to slightly screechy levels as I said the last part and my arm itched in frustration. I wanted to get away, to find a dark corner, to calm my nerves. But this guy couldn't take a hint.

Sure enough, he shook his head. "That is where you're wrong, Miss. Miller."

"Excuse me?"

"Vampires do exist."

"No, dude. They don't. Trust me. Jonathan and Maisie? I made them up."

"Yes. That is obvious. But there *are* vampires out there."

I sighed. "There are people who play at being vampires, yes. And yes, some of them drink blood. But they are not mythical creatures of the night. They're just people—really bored people."

He regarded me for a moment. As if considering what I was saying. Then he spoke. "I would like to propose a little wager," he said.

"Wager?"

"On whether vampires are real."

I laughed out loud. "Ri-ght. Sure. And what do I win if I take this bet?"

"I will donate one million dollars to RAINN. No strings attached, no questions asked."

I stared at him. "That's a lot of scratch. You sure you want to lose that much?"

"I'm not going to lose."

"Right. Okay, so let's pretend that's possible. What do you get out of the deal if you somehow manage to magically convince me there are bloodsuckers amongst us in real life?"

"One weekend."

"Excuse me?"

His eyes locked on me. "You will give me one weekend. You will come to my house. You will stay with me. And I will teach you about vampires—real vampires. And," his lips curled. "Real men."

"No way dude."

He gave me a patient look. "Don't look so shocked. You'd sleep in the spare bedroom. And I would never touch you... unless you asked me to." He chuckled. "Besides, you are positive there are no vampires, right? You're not going to lose this bet?"

He looked at me expectantly and my heart pounded in my chest. Of course he was right. There were no vampires—I was sure about that. So what did I have to lose? And to get my charity one million dollars—if he was serious! How could I pass that up?

"What kind of proof are you going to give me?" I asked. "You can't just show me someone sucking someone's blood. I mean, anyone can do that if they wanted to."

"Fine. I will not only show you. But I will convince you that vampires exist. If you are not utterly convinced by the end of tonight, I will respectfully lose the bet. I will drop you home and I will write you a check and you will never see me again."

It was ridiculous. A completely indecent proposal. And certainly nothing that someone like me would ever agree to. I mean, I was practically a recluse. I barely went to the library. I'd already been dragged out tonight against my will. And now he expected me to just take off with him—a practical stranger? So he could show me that the creatures I wrote about every day actually exist?

I opened my mouth to say no. To laugh it off. To tell him I was going back inside. But for some reason, my mouth refused to form the words, my voice stuck in my throat. His dark blue eyes drove into me, like laser beams. And I stood there, completely mute, with no idea why.

"You will come with me," he said in a deep, throaty voice, so low it made me vibrate a little inside. "Hannah."

"I'll come," I found myself saying. The opposite of what I was trying to say. Yet somehow there suddenly didn't seem another choice. I didn't know how, but I knew I would go with him. Like it was a fact, etched in stone that I was merely repeating.

His gaze softened. A small smile ghosted his lips. He made a sweeping gesture with his hand away from the party.

"My limo awaits," he said.

I raised an eyebrow. "You want to go now?" I guess I expected we'd wait until the party was over.

He didn't reply, probably because the answer would be obvious. Instead, he slipped a strong hand against the small of my back, possessively leading me down the stairs toward the parking lot.

4
_____

I peered out the window as the driver turned onto a darkened street, far away from the city center and toward a much seedier section of town. My breath fogged the pane, but I swiped it clean with my hand.

"Where are you taking me?" I asked, turning to Logan. "Transylvania?"

He snorted. "You really do know nothing about vampires, do you?"

"Are we really going to start this again?"

"I'm curious," he said. "What made you decide to write about vampires in the first place? No offense, but you don't exactly seem the type."

"What, you think you have to be goth or something?" I demanded. This wasn't the first time I had gotten this question. And, honestly, I didn't blame people for asking. I had never had much interest in horror or vampires or anything of the paranormal sort. Until the dream, that was.

"I didn't say that," Logan replied easily, stretching his arms above his head. I tried not to notice the way his shirt lifted with the movement—exposing a small ribbon of muscled flesh. He dropped his hands again and it disappeared. Which was definitely for the best. "I was just curious," he said.

"Curiosity killed the cat," I reminded him.

"Lucky for me, I'm a vampire, not a shifter."

"So there are shifters, too? Is that what you're trying to tell me?"

'The Otherworld is vast," he assured me. "There are all sort of things lurking under the skin of the world that you know. Vampires are just the beginning."

"Awesome," I muttered. This guy was deranged, I reminded myself again. Super-hot, but super insane. How had he talked me into this whole thing again?

I realized he was waiting for an answer. "It was kind of random," I said with a shrug. "And not all that interesting to be honest. One night I went to sleep. And I had a dream. About Jonathan." I paused, then added, "That's the series' hero."

He nodded. "I read the book, remember?"

"Right." I felt my face heat. Oh I remembered all right. All too well.

I cleared my throat. "Anyway in this dream he snuck into my dorm room. Clear as if I was awake. He told me his story. And he begged me to write it down." I smiled, remembering. "When I woke up, I ran to my computer. Skipped all my classes—just typed all day long. It was as if the words weren't mine. That someone—Jonathan, I guess—was whispering in my ear." I turned back to Logan. "Sorry. It sounds dumb when I try to explain out loud."

But Logan wasn't laughing. Instead, he was staring at me thoughtfully, a ponderous look in his eyes. "Had you ever written anything before?" he asked.

"A little. Short stories, mostly. Some poems. Nothing big. I mean, I never wanted to be a writer if that's what you mean," I added. "I wanted to be a librarian."

Now he laughed, his penetrating gaze raking over me. "You would have made for a very hot librarian," he teased.

I rolled my eyes. "Yeah, yeah," I said, waving him off. Though in truth I couldn't help a small trill of pleasure spiral through me. He thought I was hot? Not that I should care, but still!

"What about you?" I asked, wanting to turn the tables. "How did you become a vampire?"

To my surprise, his face darkened. As if a storm had suddenly rolled in out of nowhere. I sank back in my chair, the laughter fading from my lips. "What?"

"Are you mocking me?" he asked in a low voice.

"Uh, I was just trying to make conversation."

"You don't believe vampires exist."

"But you do," I countered. "Isn't that the whole reason I'm here? So you can convince me? Maybe if I hear your personal story..."

"No!"

His voice was sharp, angry. I clamped my mouth shut and inched away from him on my seat. Clearly I had pissed him off somehow, though I had no idea how.

"Sorry," I stammered. "I'll just shut up now."

"No," he said again, but his voice was softer this time. "We can talk. About anything you like. I want you to ask questions. That's the whole point of this exercise. So you can learn what vampires are truly like."

"But you won't tell me your story."

"My story is not interesting."

Hm. I watched him, curiously as he turned back to the window, staring intently into the black night, as if it held the secrets to the universe. The way he said that made me think it probably *was* pretty interesting. So interesting he didn't want to relate it to a stranger. Maybe it had been really traumatic for him. Like, he was turned against his will... Like in Anne Rice's

Lestat books—where his vampire sire had killed himself before explaining to Lestat how to be a vampire...

Wait. What was I thinking? I didn't believe any of this bull-shit! Logan wasn't a vampire. He was simply a deluded freak. A good looking deluded freak, I admit, but completely deluded all the same.

Because, as everyone knows, vampires simply don't exist.

Which made me wonder once again, why was I here? How did he convince me to go along with this charade? I thought back to the party. The way he'd asked. The way I'd been completely ready to say no. And then he had looked at me. With those crazy eyes of his. And suddenly I was totally on board, all in, along for the ride. Leaving my own party to go off with a strange guy without telling anyone where I was going. Sure, that was par for the course for many girls my age. But not me. I would never do something like that. I'd be too scared I'd end up being dumped in a ditch. That no one would find my body for years.

So why had I said yes? Was it simply the lure of a large chari-table donation? Or was something else going on here?

A shiver ran down my spine. One word echoing through my mind. One impossible, ridiculous word—and yet I was unable to dismiss it from my brain.

Compulsion.

Logan may have thought I knew nothing about vampires. But I knew all too well this power that vampires in TV and movies and books always seemed to have. A way to talk mortals into doing things against their will. Things they would have never agreed to do otherwise.

Could Logan have used this on me somehow? Was that how I found myself here?

I shook my head. That was ridiculous. He didn't compel me.

He just offered me a challenge. And I made a very bad, impulsive choice to accept that challenge. Period. End of story.

But for some reason, this rationalization didn't make me feel any better. And soon my arm started itching again, begging for the relief of a fingernail or blade. I was also sweating, I realized, and it was causing the thick fabric of my dress to stick to my skin. I wanted to pull my sleeve up, but, of course, I couldn't. I didn't need this guy to see the weakness written on my arms. And so instead I rubbed them with my hands, trying to feel the grooves on my skin beneath the heavy fabric. The marks of times before. Sometimes that would be enough. But right now it didn't seem to be doing much good.

"Are you all right?"

I looked up. Lost in my thoughts I hadn't realized Logan had turned away from the window. Turned back to me. He was looking at me now with what appeared to be genuine concern in his eyes. Which only made me angrier. This was all his fault, after all. Me even being here. And now he was worried about me?

"I'm fine," I spit out. "How far is this stupid place anyway?"

As if on cue, the limo stopped. Logan smiled.

"Actually, we've just arrived."

5

My mouth clamped shut. Panic flared within me. I jerked my head around to peer out the window. It was so dark it was hard to make out what was outside. I saw some lights, some movement—but it was all fleeting and blurred. Where had he taken me? And what was about to happen?

My hands clung to the car's leather seats, my heels pressing hard against the floor. I wasn't sure what I expected to achieve from this—it wasn't as if I thought he would just leave me in the limo if I suddenly decided I didn't want to go. And yet my body couldn't seem to help offering up one last fleeting show of resistance. A vain attempt to stop whatever was happening...from happening.

The door opened from the outside. The limo driver stood there, offering me a hand. For a moment, I just stared at it, my heart pounding in my chest. Then I reluctantly reached out and took it. What else could I do?

His hand was surprisingly cold. Even colder than Darla's usually were and she had terrible circulation. I allowed him to help me out of the limo, wobbling a little as my too-high heels sank into the dirt. But Logan, who had come around from the other side, grabbed me and helped me stay upright. I tried and failed not to notice how strong his hands felt against my body as he ushered me to the paved side road.

He turned to the limo driver, whispering something too low for me to hear. The driver nodded and closed the back door, then returned to his seat. I took the opportunity to look around, trying to gauge my surroundings. If I needed to run, would there be any place safe to run to? I should have paid more attention to where we were going in the car.

"Where are we?" I asked, my heart beating furiously in my chest. It was definitely a part of town I'd never seen before. The kind that no one in their right mind would want to spend time in...especially at night.

"Come," Logan said, not answering my question. He once again placed a firm hand at the small of my back, leading me away from the relative safety of the limo and down the darkened street. As we passed parked car after parked car, I could hear shouting from a not-so-far-off distance. Followed by something that sounded suspiciously like gunfire. Or fireworks?

No. Definitely gunfire.

"Are you afraid?" Logan asked softly, leaning down so his mouth was only inches from my ear. "Because, if so, you needn't be."

I shivered involuntarily as his cool breath tickled my lobe. How could this moment be so terrifying and yet so sensual, all at the same time? I tried to choke out a laugh. To break the spell. "Really? And why is that?"

"Because you're with me," Logan said simply. As if that explained everything.

I swallowed hard. Wanting desperately to believe him. Wanting to be a normal girl, out on a normal date with a normal guy. The kind of thing I used to do...before.

But that was ridiculous. I wasn't a normal girl. And this wasn't a normal date. Or a date at all, for that matter. Instead I had gone and put myself at the complete mercy of a total stranger. Something I would never, ever do.

Except, for some reason, I had.

I opened my mouth. To tell Logan I didn't want to do this. That the joke had gone too far. That I wanted to go home. That if he didn't take me home, I'd scream. I'd call the police. I'd—

My eyes fell upon the building in front of us. I squinted at it for a moment, wondering why it looked so weirdly familiar. It took me a moment, but then my eyes locked onto a small neon sign at the entrance. A sign that read: FANG.

"Wait, is this Club Fang?" I asked, curious despite myself. After all, I knew all about this place. My readers were always talking about it on my Facebook page. A lot of them were regulars. From what I could tell it was some kind of chain of clubs—goth clubs on steroids. Like, the kind of place someone would go if they fancied themselves a vampire or other creature of the night.

Or wanted to prove to a certain author that the aforementioned creatures existed, I supposed.

I let out a breath I hadn't realized I was holding, relief coursing through my veins. *I can do this,* I told myself. *It's a public place. There will be plenty of people around. Maybe some will even be readers. And there will be bouncers to step in if things get weird...*

"You know of Club Fang?" Logan asked, sounding surprised.

I turned to him. "I may be a recluse, but I still have Google."

His mouth lifted. "Of course. Silly me."

"So..." I looked around the building. "Do we just get in line?"

My eyes wandered down the line in question, which was actually absurdly long for a weird fetish club like this. Filled with goth kids dressed in black with various piercings on various appendages. Who knew we had such a large scene in our town?

I noted that a few of them were watching us curiously and at first I wondered if maybe they had recognized me from my author photo. That happened sometimes, especially in places like this. But then I realized they weren't staring at me at all. They were staring at Logan. Especially the girls.

I was surprised at the shimmer of jealousy that rippled through me as I took in their hungry eyes. I mean, how could I blame them? After all, they had no idea how pig-headed and annoying he was. They just saw a tall, hot guy with a sharp jawline and high cheekbones. I wondered what they thought of me, standing by his side, as if I had some claim over this hotness. A gothic king, escorting a plain little mouse past the line and to the front of the club.

Because, it turned out, with Logan we did not just "get in line."

In fact, when we finally reached the front door, the bouncer didn't even hesitate. He opened the red velvet rope and we stepped across the barrier as if we belonged there. Okay, fine, Logan clearly *did* belong there. But he was the only one. That said, I had to admit it was pretty cool to waltz into the club as if I was someone important. I mean, I was never a club kid, but I had seen this kind of thing many times on TV. The celebrities rolling up in their limos. The velvet ropes parting as the crowd in line seethed with jealousy. And now, for the first time in my life they were seething with jealousy over little, old me!

But all thoughts of celebrity and jealousy vanished as we stepped into the club itself. Into a treasure trove of sights and sounds that defied my craziest imagination. It was huge inside— way larger than it looked from the outside. And the dinginess of the neighborhood fell away, replaced by an opulent Victorian chic décor. Almost everything here was the color of crimson.

From the ornate velvet upholstered couches to the shiny metallic floor. Even the lights that bounced off the ceilings and walls were mostly red.

And then there was the music. Loud, dark, haunting. *Goth music*, I assumed, thinking back to when one of my fans had put together an unofficial soundtrack for Maisie and Jonathan. Which, at the time, I had found pretty amusing; after all, Maisie and Jonathan may have been vampires, but they were definitely not goths. In fact, Maisie had a thing for Taylor Swift. And Jonathan? Well, he liked old school. Like *really* old school. Bach, Beethoven...

"So," I said, trying to raise my voice to be heard over the music. "This is a vampire club?"

Logan shrugged. "Partially," he said. "They allow humans to come here, too."

"What, as hors d'oeuvres?" I couldn't help but quip.

He frowned, looking a little insulted. "As *customers*," he corrected, stiffly. "There aren't enough vampires to keep the place open on its own. Not to mention vampires hardly ever pay a cover."

"Of course they don't." I resisted the urge to roll my eyes.

I looked around the club, trying to take it all in. The place was packed with goth kids (and vampires posing as goth kids?) dancing to the beat. The dance they were doing looked something akin to having one's foot stuck in a mud puddle. They'd carefully remove the foot, lifting it up into the air, then setting it back down again, only to repeat the movement with the other foot. Meanwhile their arms were going wild, waving in the air, as if they were some weird brand of sorcerers casting a spell.

"So...who are the vampires?" I asked. "They all look alike to me."

Logan scanned the room for a moment before answering. "I think everyone out here is mortal," he said. "Vampires don't always come out to the main floor. They usually prefer...the back rooms."

I tried to suppress a shiver running down my spine. The way he said "back rooms" sounded menacing, though I wasn't sure why. Most clubs, after all, had a VIP room, right? Well, maybe this was a VIV room—for very important vampires who didn't wish to mingle with mortals.

"So what's in the back room?" I asked, against my better judgement.

He smiled. "Come," he said. "And I will show you."

And so I followed him through the crowd, trying my best to dodge all the dancers and those carrying drinks. I had to admit, it looked like a pretty fun club—if you were into this sort of scene. I would have to tell my readers next time I went online that I had come here to check it out. They would be so excited. After all, they wanted nothing more than for me to be one of them. For once I wouldn't disappoint.

Finally, we reached a back door, guarded by another bouncer. This guy was even bigger and burlier than the one outside—who had been pretty intimidating in and of himself. But he only smiled when he saw Logan and I, reaching out and opening the door.

"It's good to see you again, Sir," he said, addressing Logan with a stiff bow. "It has been far too long."

Logan gave him a respectful nod of his head in return. "Good to see you, too, Francis," he said. "My duties for the Blood Coven have kept me quite occupied." He smiled. "No time for getting my groove on."

"Blood Coven? What the heck is a Blood Coven?" I asked as we stepped through the door. Logan waited for it to close behind us before turning back to me.

"A coven is a vampire's family," he explained. "They are also a political entity that resides under the jurisdiction of a larger vampire consortium, made up of coven representatives that decide the laws of the land."

"You guys have an actual government?" I asked. "That's pretty hardcore."

"Pretty *necessary*," he corrected. "If we are to survive as a species and live amongst humans, we need to retain law and order amongst our kind."

"Sure," I said, resisting the urge to roll my eyes again. It was crazy how serious these people took this game. I mean I've seen some pretty intense fandoms, but this was on another level entirely.

We walked down a hallway, painted (predictably) all in red. The further we got, the more nervous I started to feel and my hands began to tremble. Back in the club I felt relatively safe, surrounded by people. Now I was once again alone with a guy who seemed to truly believe he was part of some vampire cult. What was I going to find at the end of this hallway? And would I ever be allowed to leave?

Finally, the hallway ended, opening up into a large waiting room. At least it looked like a waiting room, complete with couches and coffee tables and magazines. There was even a receptionist, sitting behind a desk, reading a novel. And each wall had multiple doors. Like little booths or something.

I frowned. "What is this?" I asked.

Logan gave me a wicked smile. "The dining room," he replied.

"The *what*?"

"Where vampires feed?"

Ew. I wrinkled my nose, realizing what he was implying. I had tried to tell myself that maybe these vampire wannabes didn't actually go so far as to drink actual blood. But who was I kidding? Of course they drank it.

"So, what? You drag humans back here and suck them dry?"

I asked, my stomach starting to feel quite queasy. I really hoped I wouldn't suddenly be told I was on tonight's menu.

He snorted. "It's a bit more regulated than that," he said.

"Regulated blood sucking? Now that's a first."

"Actually it's been practiced for years," he corrected. "I mean, think about it. You can't just grab someone off the street and drain them dry. Who knows what kind of blood diseases they may be carrying?"

"Also, you know, there's the whole first degree murder thing," I added.

He laughed. "Yes. Also it's murder," he agreed. "And if the cops started finding a bunch of dead bodies in alleyways, drained of blood, they might start getting suspicious."

"So...where do you get your blood then?" I asked, praying he was going to say steak bought from the local butcher. But in my heart I knew I wasn't going to be that lucky.

"From donors," he explained instead. "People who we contract to give regular blood donations. After a strict vetting process, of course. Lots of testing."

"Uh, why would anyone sign up for that?"

He shrugged. "We pay very well. It's actually quite a good part time job. Great for single moms, for example. They can set their own hours, don't have to deal with day care."

I let out a low whistle. They really had an answer for everything, didn't they? "Good to know if I ever need some extra cash," I joked. "Just open a vein and start printing money."

To my surprise, Logan's face fell. He gave me a disappointed look. "You still don't believe," he said. It wasn't a question.

"Believe people are sucking other people's blood in here?" I asked. "No. I definitely believe that. I even believe you pay them for the privilege." I added. "Hell, I know plenty of my more... serious...fans do the whole bloodletting thing. And, honestly, it's great to know you screen people first because I always thought it seemed like a really risky thing to do.

"But," I continued, "Do I think these people here are actual vampires? Immortal, all-powerful creatures who need blood to survive?" I shook my head. "Sorry, but no."

He nodded, still looking disappointed, but at the same time, not surprised. As if he expected this answer. It made me wonder, suddenly, if this was part of his overall plan. He had to know, deep down, that real vampires didn't exist, right? And therefore he had to know he'd never actually convince me. Which meant he had to have some other motive for bringing me here. Like, maybe this was some convoluted pretense to get me out on a date. After all, he had to know there was no way I'd agree to any of this otherwise.

It was pretty brazen, if it were true. And pretty complicated, too. But then the alternative—that he actually believed in vampires? That was even more ridiculous.

I frowned, the new theory annoying me more than I wanted to admit. I mean, here I was, in the middle of nowhere, in the middle of the night. Surrounded by a bunch of freaks who got their rocks off drinking people's blood. Was this my penance for writing the books I did? After all, my novels celebrated this kind of behavior. Made it seem cool—romantic even. But now, as I watched a couple of junkie looking teens, pale and malnourished, limp from the bloodletting rooms and collapse on the couch, I felt a little nauseated. Was I the cause of any of this?

Maybe I needed to switch to detective novels for my next book...

Logan's gaze bore down on me. "A little too real for you?"

I winced. "Can we just...go back to the main room? I think I've seen enough."

He nodded and led me out of the room, down the hall, and through the door, back into the club. By this point the music had changed. From the moody goth to a more electronic beat. Fast, driving. In other situations, I might have thought it kind of cool. Now I was too frazzled. And I found myself glancing longingly at the bar.

Logan caught my gaze. "Need a drink, huh?" he asked.

"Is it that obvious?"

He grabbed my hand, leading me over to the bar. We sat down on the stools and I ordered a Moscow Mule. He got a glass of Cabernet. I eyed his drink suspiciously as the bartender set it down in front of him.

"Is that blood?"

He laughed. "Blood of the gods," he teased. Then he pushed his glass in my direction. "It's wine," he told me. "Taste it if you like."

I leaned over to sniff his drink. Sure enough it smelled like wine. I let out a breath of relief.

"Sorry," I said. "It's just...well, this has been a weird night."

"I should be the one to apologize," he said. "Dragging you out here like this."

I waved my hand. "Honestly, it's more interesting than that stuffy charity event. No offense."

He laughed. A rich, deep, throaty laugh. "Fair enough."

I bit my lower lip. "Did you...really just plan that whole thing to get my attention?"

"It worked, didn't it?"

"So does email. And it doesn't cost thirty thousand dollars."

"I don't do email."

"Oh right. Cause you're a thousand-year-old vampire. I forgot."

He sighed. "I haven't convinced you of anything, have I?"

I gave him a rueful look. 'Sorry."

"It's all right," he said, reaching out and taking my hand in his, stroking it gently. I swallowed hard. I knew I should pull away, but at the same time it felt kind of nice. Which was crazy, but there you go.

"You don't really think you're a vampire, do you?" I asked. "I mean, all this was just a ruse, right? To get me to go out with you?"

He looked up, surprised. "Is that what you think?"

"I don't know. Maybe?" I paused, then added. "It makes more sense than the alternative."

"It does," he agreed, squeezing my hand lightly. I tried not to squirm as chills ran up and down my arms. "There's just...something about you, Hannah. I saw it the moment you walked into that bookstore. It was the oddest feeling. Like I had to meet you." He shrugged. "It was a very unfamiliar feeling and it irritated me greatly at first."

"Was that why you were such an asshole?"

His mouth curled. "You thought I was an asshole?"

"Dude. You accused me of not knowing anything about vampires...or men for that matter!"

"Right." Logan groaned. Then he shook his head. "I'm sorry, Hannah," he said, meeting my eyes with his own. "And I'm sorry I said I didn't like your book. Truth is, well, I actually did like it."

My eyes widened. This, I was not expecting. "What?"

Even under the club's dim lighting I could see his face darken to a rosy blush. "Don't get me wrong. I *wanted* to hate it," he confessed. "I really did. But it was...compelling. I don't know how else to explain. I literally couldn't put it down."

A thrill of triumph spun down my spine, even though I knew it was totally petty. "You should put that in your GoodReads review," I teased.

He laughed. "Alongside my reviews of Proust and Dostoyevsky?"

"You are such a snob."

"And you are a good writer. Don't let any vampire tell you differently."

"Can I put that on the cover of my next book?"

"I insist on it."

I grinned. "I guess you're not *such* an asshole after all."

"And yet you're still beautiful." Logan stood up, not letting go of my hand. "Dance with me, Hannah."

Before I could respond, he pulled at my hand, dragging me out onto the dance floor. I stumbled after him, my mind still stuck on his last comment. Did he just call me beautiful?

"Wait!" I cried. "You never said anything about dancing,"

He stopped in his tracks. Turned to face me. His eyes were flashing with mischief. "You ran out on our last dance," he reminded me. "You owe me."

I swallowed hard, my heart racing in my chest. I opened my mouth—to say something, anything to protest. Instead I found myself letting him take me into his arms. His strong hands gripping my waist. His eye remaining locked on me, their hold seemingly as powerful as his grip. I tried to squirm away, to put some distance between us, but somehow my body refused to obey and instead I found myself pressed up against him. My soft curves melting into his hard planes.

I placed my head on his shoulder, breathing in his warm, rich scent. He smelled like mixture of juniper and fir with a hint of something at first I couldn't identify, but was oddly reminiscent of an ancient library. That comforting smell of books with yellowed pages. I had always loved the smell of old books. A soothing scent that reminded me of home.

What are you doing? my frenzied brain demanded. But I pushed it away. I knew it was wrong. Stupid, even. But it had been so long since I'd allowed myself to be touched. For a moment I just wanted to be like everyone else. A normal girl who didn't shrink away from a hot guy. In that moment I didn't want to think about vampires and what was real. I just wanted to lose myself in the moment. In the music's driving beat. In Logan's rich, delicious smell.

And so we danced. As if we were the only people in the room. As if this were completely normal. Completely natural. And when the song ended, we didn't break apart. Instead, Logan reached up, brushing a lock of hair out of my eyes and it was all I could do not to collapse as the chills spun down my spine. I tried to catalog the sensations pouring through me. Stow them away to use in a book later.

For, indeed, this moment felt like a book. Though Logan was nothing like Jonathan. Sure, he resembled him physically, but at the same time he exuded a far different power, a raw masculinity that Jonathan could never hope to achieve. Jonathan was a gentleman. Logan was more of a predator. Taking what he wanted without bothering to ask permission first.

Speaking of... His eyes bore down on me, flashing with inner fire. I could have sworn they had been blue, but now they looked more like purple in the dim club lights. Cupping my face in his hands, he tilted my head up so I was forced to meet his eyes with my own. I gasped at the look of raw power I saw on his face. The lust in his gaze. He smiled greedily, then leaned in for the kill.

Or in this case, kiss.

I nearly fainted as his mouth brushed against mine. His tongue darting out, licking the seam of my lips. Chills ransacked my body, rendering me helpless in his arms.

I had written a billion kisses in my novels. I knew all the creative ways to describe tongues and mouths and lips. But this —this was something I couldn't put into words if I tried. It was like it took over, stealing away my ability to think. And as Logan groaned against my mouth, I realized suddenly that this wasn't a one-way street either. I was having as much an effect on him as he was on me. The thought filled me with a raw, surging sense of power. A power I hadn't felt in a long time. Maybe ever.

"Hannah," he moaned against my mouth. "Oh Hannah..."

It was then that I felt it. A tiny prick against my tongue. A sudden heat.

What the hell?

I jerked away, lifting my hand to my mouth as pain radiated through me, sharp and pulsing. When I pulled my hand away, I found blood pooling in my palm.

"What...?" I whispered. I looked up at Logan, confused as hell. "Did you just...bite me?" Horror coursed through me as I waited for an answer. An answer I was pretty sure I didn't want to hear.

He gave me a distraught look. "I'm sorry," he said. "You just felt so good. I didn't mean..."

"Oh my God. You sick fuck!" I cried, stumbling backward, putting distance between us. My mouth was stinging now, as if I'd just swallowed a gob of wasabi.

"I didn't bite you," Logan said, taking a cautious step toward me. "You just nicked your tongue on my fang."

"You don't have fangs," I spit out. After all, I'd seen him smile half a dozen times tonight. I would have noticed if he had vampire teeth.

He gave me an apologetic look. Then he opened his mouth, baring his teeth. My eyes widened in horror as I saw two glittering fangs.

"But...but..." I stammered. "Those weren't there! When did you put them in?" My mind raced for a moment when he could have turned away from me. Slipped them in his mouth when I wasn't looking. But I came up blank.

Logan sighed. "They're not always visible," he explained. "They only come out when..." He looked sheepish. "When I... get excited."

My face burned at his insinuation. He might have just told me I'd given him an erection. A tooth erection. My stomach wrenched and my knees practically gave out from under me. My eyes darted around the club, at all the other patrons, dressed in black, pretending to be in some kind of vampire den. This was so sick. This was truly sick. I needed to get out of here. Now.

"Hannah..."

"I have to pee!" I blurted out. The only thing I could think of at the moment—the only place he couldn't follow. Not waiting for his reply I turned and bolted across the dance floor, as fast as my legs could carry me toward the sign that read *bathroom*. But when I reached it, I didn't go inside.

I didn't have to go. I had to get out.

The front door was in the other direction, but my eyes spotted an exit near the back of the club. For smokers, I guessed. Or for those who needed a breath of fresh air. I dove for the door, as if my life depended on it, pissing off a few patrons as I pushed past them in the process.

What had I been thinking? Agreeing to any of this? Going off to a strange place with a guy who thought he was a vampire? Agreeing to dance with him. Allowing him to kiss me. This was exactly the reason I avoided these types of establishments in the first place. So I couldn't get myself in these situations.

If you just let me escape this, I begged silently to any higher power who might be listening. *I'll never go out again.*

I pushed through the door, out into a back alley. It slammed shut behind me and I realized it was one of those doors you could leave out of, but you couldn't get back through. Which was more than fine by me. I had no interest in returning. In running into Logan and his weird dental work again.

I leaned against the brick wall, sucking in a much needed breath. My mouth had stopped stinging, thank God, but my heart was going a mile a minute. What had happened in there?

Had Logan really sprouted fangs? That was impossible, of course. But I saw no other explanation.

I will not only show you. I will convince you vampires are real.

His words echoed through my head sending a shiver down my spine. I had to admit, I was almost convinced. And yet, at the same, more confused than ever.

There was only one thing left to do. I reached into my bag and pulled out my blade.

_____

he small blade flashed under the street lights, sending relief flooding through my brain. Just seeing it there, feeling it between my fingers, was already working to calm me down. Half the time it was just knowing that the release was coming. That soon it would all be okay.

Leaning against the brick wall, I exhaled, then took a deep breath, trying to steady my heartbeat and still my shaky hands. Then, in one fluid motion, I brought the razor to my arm, slicing across my skin. Just a small cut—nothing major. Nothing that would require a huge bandage. Just a thin crimson ribbon slipping across my forearm, offering the panic a means of escape. I let out a second breath and closed my eyes. Feeling so much better already.

That was until the door burst open with a loud bang, shattering my reverie. I leaped from the wall, panic rising through me all over again, at first thinking it must be Logan coming to find me.

But it wasn't Logan. It was someone else entirely. A young man, tall and lithe and dressed all in black. He had long brown hair falling over strange silver colored eyes. Not bad looking, mind you. Though nothing compared to Logan. (But, then, only few could even hope for that.)

I watched, a little nervous, as the man stood there for a moment. His brow furrowed and his posture tense. He cocked his head, seeming to sniff the air.

Then his head snapped in my direction.

Fear gripped my heart as he started stalking toward me. His lips curled in a feral snarl. I looked behind me, hoping there was someone else there—some other target. But we were alone. He was coming for me.

My gaze darted around, desperate to locate an escape. But we were at the end of an alley and he was standing between me and the only exit. I started to back away anyway, trying to think, trying to rationalize what was happening. But all my frantic brain could come up with was the last time I'd been cornered by a guy.

A guy I knew. A guy I had agreed to be with.

This man—this man was...

He grabbed me. Literally lifted me off my feet, slamming me against the brick wall. I screamed and struggled to get away— but he was too strong. And when I landed a kick between his legs, he didn't even seem to notice. Instead, he grabbed my arm with a force that almost snapped it in two. I bellowed in pain, tears streaming down my cheeks.

"Let me go!" I begged. "You can have my purse—I've got money!"

But he didn't answer. Instead, to my absolute horror, he brought my arm to his mouth and started licking it. Sliding his thick, slimy tongue along the bloody cut I'd just made.

"Oh my God," I whispered. "Please. *Please* don't."

I tried to squirm away again, but he slammed his fist into my stomach, making me double over in pain. His mouth was now securely locked onto my arm and I could almost feel the blood being sucked from my veins.

Because he's a vampire, my frantic brain lectured. *A real life vampire.*

And he was about to drain me dry.

7
───────

"*P*lease!" I begged as the vampire continued to suck at my arm. "Please let me go! You can have whatever you want! This necklace is worth at least ten-thousand dollars..."

But I might as well have been arguing with a wall. He didn't want a necklace. He wanted my blood. And it seemed there was nothing I could bargain with that would take that want away.

How ironic, I thought as my head began to spin. I was already starting to weaken thanks to the blood loss and I wondered how long I would be able to stay standing. *I made my fortune off writing vampires. Now I would die with a purse full of money—and not a drop of blood left.*

My knees buckled, giving out from under me. I dropped to the ground, tears streaming down my cheeks. The light around me seemed to be fading and I was starting to feel so tired. I just wanted to fall asleep and—

"Hannah!"

The club door flew open again and I vaguely heard a voice calling out my name. I looked up, the landscape swimming before my eyes. It took me a moment to register who it was.

Logan.

He looked down, taking one moment to assess the scene. Then he grabbed the vampire, ripping him off of me. Blood splattered onto the pavement and onto my dress, but I barely noticed as I watched Logan slam the vampire against the wall. The creature snarled at him, revealing his fangs, still dripping with my blood. But Logan held him by the neck, his eyes flashing fire and his own fangs bared.

He turned to me. "Run, Hannah. Get to the limo. Quickly!"

I did my best to nod, to let him know I understood. I couldn't even speak at this point, it felt like too much effort and I felt too weak to do much more than crawl. My mind was spinning, my head aching, but I forced myself to focus on the task in front of me. To get to the limo. To get away.

At last I managed to rise to my feet, using the wall for support. Behind me I could still hear the two vampires fighting, but I forced myself not to turn around. Instead, I limped toward the exit, focusing on freedom shining from a street lamp—literally the light at the end of a tunnel.

I almost made it. But then something compelled me to turn around. To see how the fight was going. If Logan had beaten the other vampire yet. To my dismay I saw just the opposite. The vampire had Logan on the ground and was slamming his beautiful face in with his fist.

Shit.

I bit my lower lip, my mind racing with fear. If he killed Logan—or even knocked him out—he'd be coming after me next. He'd finish me off for good.

I should run. I should get into the limo before that happened. Speed away.

But then... Logan had saved my life. How could I just turn my back on him. Let him die. That would be selfish. Cruel. Though, on the other hand, what could I possibly do to help?

Little old me was not going to even make a dent in Big Vampire Baddie.

Unless...

Suddenly, an idea struck me like a jolt of lightning. The rosary beads! The ones the fan had given me at my last signing. Darla had put them in my purse. They were probably still there. Could they help somehow? They always seemed to work in the movies...

I made the decision before I even realized I was making it. Reaching into my bag, I grabbed the beads in my fist. Then, channeling all my remaining strength I rushed at the two vampires. Logan was still on the ground and the other vampire was trying to slash his neck with his fangs. Thankfully he was so engrossed in doing so he didn't see me.

"Take that, you asshole!" I cried, pressing the cross against his left cheek.

"ARRRRR!"

The vampire howled, jerking his head. I watched in fascinated horror as his skin seemed to sizzle where the cross had touched it. His flesh burning up. His hands dropped from Logan's neck and flew to his face.

Which was all the advantage Logan needed. He flipped the man over, grabbing an abandoned piece of rebar in his hand. He raised it up, then let it come down. Staking the vampire through the heart.

The vampire burst into a pile of dust. Like literally exploded before my eyes. Just like in the movies. But in real life.

I screamed, dropping to my knees again. The rosary beads slipped from my hands and fell to the ground.

"Oh my God," I cried. "Oh my GOD!"

Logan turned to me. His face was ashen and his clothes filthy. "We need to get out of here," he said, his voice hoarse and scratchy. "His friends won't be far behind."

I nodded, unable to speak. Logan stalked over to me, grabbing me and lifting me into his arms, as if I weighed nothing at all. Then, to my shock, he bent his knees, then pushed off the ground, launching us into the air. A moment later we were twenty feet off the ground. Then thirty. Then...

We were flying. Legit vampire flying.

"You know," I said, as my head started spinning again, darkness swimming before my eyes. I snuggled against his chest, breathing in his rich, deep scent. "If you really wanted to prove the whole vampire thing you might have just led with the fact that you can fly. Just saying..."

I could feel his smile against the top of my head. "I'll keep that in mind for next time," he said.

"Next time?" I started to ask. "You think you're getting a second date?"

I passed out before I could hear his answer.

8

I woke up hours later in an unfamiliar bed. For a moment I couldn't remember what had happened; my brain felt as if it had been stuffed with cotton. My head hurt, too. A pounding, rhythmic ache. And I felt so weak and exhausted—as if I'd been hit by a truck or something. And then there was the ache at my wrist...

I shot up in bed, my eyes dropping to my arm. To the small cut, framed by large bite marks.

Fang marks.

My heart pounded in my chest as the memories of the night before flooded back to me. It felt like a nightmare, like a dream I was waking from. But the marks on my wrist told me it was all too real.

I looked around the room, wondering where I was. Where Logan had taken me. I remember him taking flight. (Taking FLIGHT!) I remembered resting my head on his chest. Breathing in his rich, dark scent. Listening for his heartbeat before remembering that, as a vampire, he wouldn't have one. After that I must have passed out.

My first observation was that the room was empty. Logan the

vampire was nowhere to be found. My second observation was of the sun, streaming through a large window. It was daylight. The time all good vampires must go to bed.

The room itself was luxurious. The bed ridiculously soft and the sheets and duvet were crisp and clean. And there were understated, elegant furnishings, like what one might find in a model home. Unlike the crimson coated Club Fang this room was done up in light blues and soft grays. About as un-vampire as you could get—if you believed the clichés.

Ugh.

I groaned, rubbing my head with my hands. So I guess I had to really go with this now. The realization that this whole vampire thing was the real deal. After all, how could I argue otherwise? I'd seen a man's face burn after being marked by a crucifix. I watched him being staked through the heart and poofed into dust. And then there was the flying thing. That was a tough one to explain without first accepting the paranormal nature of the flyer in question.

I shook my head, trying to still my rapid heartbeat. The last thing I needed right now was to panic. I had to figure out where I was and how I would get home. How I could return to normal life and leave all this crazy behind.

I swung my feet over the side of the bed and slipped to the floor. My toes sank into the plush carpet and for a moment I just stood there, trying to steady myself. I could definitely tell I'd lost quite a bit of blood the night before.

It was then that I noticed I wasn't wearing my old clothes. The itchy, uncomfortable long-sleeve dress I had donned the night before was nowhere to be seen. Instead, I was wearing a soft gray t-shirt that was so large it fell to my knees and a pair of plaid pajama pants. I looked around the room again, trying to locate any of my belongings, but saw nothing I recognized. Awesome.

I headed to the door, figuring maybe he'd left my stuff outside. Maybe my dress had blood on it and he threw it in the wash. It should have been dry-cleaned, of course, but I wasn't about to quibble over dress laundering right now. Not when Logan had literally saved my life.

I at least needed to find my phone. To call Darla and let her know I was okay. After that, I could figure out the rest.

My hand wrapped around the doorknob. I tried to turn it. But it held fast. It was then that I noticed the keyhole just below.

Oh no.

Panic seized me with icy fingers. I ran to the room's window, trying to yank it open. But it seemed to be painted shut. I looked around the room, desperate to find something that would allow me to break the glass—like you always see people in movies do when they're trapped. But then I noticed the iron bars just outside the window. Even if I did manage to break glass, I wasn't going anywhere.

I was trapped.

In the house of a real life vampire.

I sank down to the carpet, tears welling in my eyes. Why did he lock me in? Was he going to make me his prisoner? How long would he keep me? Was the only reason he saved me last night because I was on tonight's menu?

I felt the blood pulse in my arm, desperate to be unleashed. I looked around the room again, for something I could use as a blade. I needed relief—even just a moment's relief from the panic spiraling through me. Scrambling to my feet, I searched the room. Emptying drawers, looking under the bed. Hoping for something—anything—that might work in a pinch.

It was then that I found the note.

Dearest Hannah,

I beg your forgiveness for the night before. I never meant for
any of this to happen. I only wanted to introduce you to my
world. And yet instead it appears I have brought you into a
nightmare.

I know you're probably frightened, but rest assured that you
are safe in this house. I am so sorry to have had to lock you in
your room, but I promise you it's for your own protection. I will
be there to release you the second the sun sets tonight. That is
a promise.

In the meantime, there are snacks in the mini fridge in the
closet and some drinks. And I've left you a laptop in case you
would like to use the time to write. I know you said you were
under deadline and I don't want to be the cause of you getting
further behind.

Yours,
    Logan

I CRUMPLED the note in my hand and threw it across the room,
anxiety and nausea welling up inside of me. At least I knew he
wasn't planning on saving me for a midnight snack, I supposed.
But the thought didn't make me feel all that much better. I was
still stuck here. Still trapped. Still under the grip of a deadly
creature of the night.

For a while I just sat there, staring at the wall, wondering
what I should do. But eventually the overwhelming fear settled
to a dull ache and I found myself less frightened and more
bored. Also hungry. I scrambled to my feet and headed over to

the closet to investigate the minibar situation. As promised it was filled with various snacks and sodas. I popped open a Diet Coke and took a sip. Then I grabbed a can of Pringles and sat down in front of the laptop.

I turned it on, at first holding out hope it might have some sort of Wi-Fi. But, of course, it was password protected. I tried a few half-hearted attempts at guessing the password, but eventually just signed into Microsoft Word. Judging from the position of the sun in the sky I had many hours to wait in this room. And writing was the only thing that would help pass the time.

"Okay Jonathan," I whispered to the blank page. "Let's do this."

*a*t first I wasn't sure I'd even be able to write. Trapped in this strange place, my life likely literally in danger. But somehow, to my surprise, I was able to dive right in. Lose myself in the story. In fact, I wrote all afternoon and when I finally heard the knock at the door, I looked up, shocked to realize hours had passed since I sat down. The window outside was pitch black.

Night had fallen.

The knock came again. "Um, come in?" I stammered, not sure what to say. My pulse skittered at my wrist as my nerves amped up with a vengeance.

I heard a clicking sound, a key being inserted into a lock. Then the door squeaked open and Logan stepped into the room.

I drew in a breath. Logan. The vampire who had kidnapped me. Who'd kept me locked up all day. And yet looking at him now, I felt such a rush of relief. Which was crazy, right? I mean, I should be furious with the guy—and I was! I really was. But at the same time I couldn't help this weird feeling of gratitude. He had saved my life last night. Though, to be fair, he was the one who had put it in danger to begin with.

Also, he was carrying a plate with a piece of yummy smelling pizza on it. He set it down on the desk. "I thought you might be hungry," he said.

I looked down at the gooey cheese, sorely tempted to shove the entire thing in my mouth. Despite the snacks I was starving for real food. But in the end I managed to restrain myself. Taking the pizza would be telling Logan everything was okay. And this was definitely not okay.

"You need to let me go," I said, rising to my feet. "Now."

I started to the door, not waiting for his answer. But he was too quick, moving at a speed I could barely catalog with my eyes. Like one instant he was at the desk. The next he stood in front of the door, blocking my path.

Vampires, man.

"I'm sorry," he said, to his credit looking quite contrite. "But that's impossible."

Anger, mixed with a healthy dose of fear, rose inside me. "You can't just keep me here!" I protested.

"I have no choice," he replied. "They're out looking for us. If they find us they will take us in—or worse."

I raked a frustrated hand through my curls, trying to keep my composure. I had no idea, of course, what he was talking about and half of me wanted to demand answers. The other half didn't want to give him the satisfaction. Didn't want to play into all his games. I just wanted to go home. To my old life. My small, cozy apartment. My poor hungry cat.

"Look, I believe you, okay?" I said, deciding to try a different tact. "You win the bet. Vampires exist. I'm utterly convinced. And they're nothing like the creatures in my book." I paused, looking up to meet his eyes with my own. "So can I go now?"

He groaned. "Hannah, I'm so sorry," he said. "I never meant for you to get hurt. I just thought it would be fun to show you my world. To freak you out a little and maybe give you a little fodder for your next book. I never thought..." he shook his head mournfully.

"Never thought what?"

He turned back to me, his eyes dark and serious. "How much do you remember about last night?" he asked. "About what happened after you ran outside the club."

I shrugged uneasily. "I ended up in an alley. And this vampire attacked me out of nowhere."

Not exactly out of nowhere, my mind niggled. *You cut yourself. He was attracted to your blood.*

But no way was I mentioning that pesky little detail to Logan.

Logan paced the room, his steps eating up the distance between walls. I looked longingly at the door, now unguarded. Should I try to make a run for it? But no, he'd catch up to me in a heartbeat.

"It's so strange," he muttered. "Why would he bite you?"

"Duh. Cause he's a vampire."

He shook his head. "Contrary to popular belief most vampires don't just attack random people. Remember what I told you at the club? We have licensed blood donors who are well paid for their services."

I nodded, remembering. "Maybe he was out of cash and forgot his ATM card?"

Or maybe some stupid girl went and opened up a vein for him.

Yes, I was the ultimate idiot, wasn't I? Cutting myself outside a vampire bar, of all places. Though, to be fair, I hadn't yet realized that vampires were a real thing.

"Anyway, he's dead now," I reminded Logan. "So what's the big deal?"

Logan turned to me, his eyes flashing fire. "What's the big deal?" he repeated. "Are you kidding me? A vampire is dead. By my own hand."

"Oh. Right." I pursed my lips. "I suppose you have laws about murder, too, huh?" That hadn't actually crossed my mind.

"Very strict laws," he said. "And when his coven finds out what we did, they will be out for blood. And if they find us, they will have every right to kill us in revenge."

I sank down onto the bed, staring at my hands. "Oh," was all I could manage to say. But inside my mind was racing with terror. One vampire had been bad enough. Now we were essentially on the run from an entire coven of them? Would I ever get back to my real life?

"This is a disaster," Logan moaned. "A total disaster."

"But couldn't we just tell them it was self-defense?" I suggested. "I mean I was minding my own business. And he shows up and starts chomping on my arm! He would have drained me dry if you hadn't shown up. Doesn't that count for something?"

Logan nodded absently, still looking distressed. He ran a hand through his tousled hair and I tried and failed not to notice how the black strands fell through his long fingers. Suddenly I was back at the club, my body pressed up against his, his mouth moving against my own. Why, oh why had I gone and run away? Sure, I'd been freaked out about the whole making out with a vamp thing. But that was way less bothersome than being a fugitive, on the run from pissed off paranormal creatures of the night.

Logan groaned, dropping down into a nearby chair. "I'm sorry," he said. "Trust me--I never meant to drag you into any of this. But now you're a part of it, whether you like it or not. By now they'll have reviewed the video footage from the cameras outside the club. Maybe even sent it to Slayer Inc."

I raised an eyebrow. "Slayer *what*?"

"Slayer *Inc.*," Logan repeated. "Basically a police force for the otherworldly creatures on this Earth. The Consortium made a deal with them a long time ago, to help us live peacefully amongst humans and other paranormal creatures. If a crime is committed—like a murder, for example—they'll get a commission to track the perpetrator down and take him out."

I made a face. So now I had to worry about a vampire coven *and* a group of Buffy wannabes? This was sounding more and more like a plot from one of my books. And not one I wanted to live in real life.

Anger rose inside of me, a desperate attempt to squash my fear. "So now what?" I demanded. "I'm supposed to just stay here, at your house, forever then?"

"No." He shook his head. "It won't be forever. Just until I can arrange a meeting with the Consortium House Speaker, Magnus. We'll go to him and we'll explain what happened. He's said to be very fair. He's also the former Master of the Blood Coven so we have that at least."

"Lucky us."

He gave me a rueful smile. "In the meantime, is there anything I can do to make you more comfortable?"

"I think you've done enough," I snapped.

His smile faded. A shadow crossed over his face. He rose to his feet. "Right," he said stiffly. 'Well, let me know if you change your mind."

"I'm good thanks," I muttered, dropping my gaze so as not to look at the hurt I caught in his eyes. *He saved your life,* something inside me nagged. *And now he's putting his own life at risk to shelter you. Maybe a little gratitude?*

I shook my head, pushing the voice away. Maybe he had saved my life. But without him my life wouldn't have been in danger to begin with. He had compelled me to come against my will. If he hadn't, I would have been safe and sound at home, sipping tea and writing the latest chapter. Because of him my life had been turned upside down.

So no. Gratitude was so not going to happen. Not on my watch. And no sad puppy dog eyes were going to change that.

"Now if you'll excuse me, I'm right in the middle of a chapter," I said, gesturing to my laptop. Total lie, of course. But all I could think of to say. I needed him out of the room before I changed my mind. Before I tried to seek comfort from the enemy.

"Very well," he said, picking up the uneaten plate of pizza.

My stomach panged in protest; I'd been hoping he'd leave it there when he left. And while I knew he still would if I opened my mouth to ask him, my pride was too great to beg. I might be stuck here, but I refused to grovel for favors at his feet.

"I have some calls to make," he added. "Shall we rendezvous in the dining room in an hour?"

I looked up, surprised. "You're not locking me in my room?"

"No. Now that you've been made aware of the situation, you're free to roam the house. You're welcome to use anything you find. TV, books. I have a well-stocked library. And if there's anything you do need, please don't hesitate to ask."

"How about a cell phone?" I said automatically.

He sighed. "Anything but that. We cannot risk contact with the outside world. It's too dangerous."

I groaned. "Why did I have a feeling you'd say that?"

10

I worked for an hour, but didn't get much done. Turned out it was tough to write about vampires when one was suddenly living amongst them. My mind kept fleeing back to the scene at the nightclub. But strangely it wasn't the attack itself that kept niggling at my brain. But rather the moments just before—when I was dancing with Logan.

Or more specifically when I was kissing Logan.

You cannot tell me that was not the most thrilling night of your life, that pesky voice inside me nagged again.

Oh God. I groaned, leaning back in my chair. I had to stop. Now. Since clearly I was already suffering from Stockholm Syndrome my first day of being kidnapped against my will. I mean, it had to be that, right? There's no other way I'd be interested in a guy like that—never mind a vampire who had literally abducted me.

Saved my life.

I gave up. Rose from my seat. Headed out of my room to explore the rest of the house. As I passed room after opulent room, I became more and more impressed. The place was huge. And all of it as well appointed as my bedroom. Not in the over-the-top Victorian décor way the club had been. But simple and elegant. There was even a small theater and a game room with pool tables and video games from the 1980s. I had to admit, if I had to be stuck somewhere, it might as well be here.

It took me a bit, but I finally found the dining room. One place setting had been set up on the table. Fine china and real looking silver. A glass half filled with wine. I thought back to my mismatched sets of forks and spoons at home. Then again, I supposed vampires had all the time in the universe to accumulate the world's luxuries. And I suddenly wondered how old Logan actually was. In the movies and books vampires were always super old. Like thousands of years. Which always struck me as a little creepy. Especially when they'd give their hearts to teenage girls.

"How did the writing go?"

I nearly jumped out of my skin as the voice shivered down my back. I whirled around to find Logan standing there behind me. I hadn't heard him approach. Another vampire thing, I guessed.

"Um, fine," I stammered. I never liked to talk about my work in progress. It felt invasive. Like someone catching me only half-dressed. I glanced at the table. "So, about that pizza…"

He frowned. "I threw that away. You didn't seem interested."

My stomach growled angrily. *Thanks a lot,* it seemed to be saying. I sighed. "I don't suppose you have anything else to eat, do you?" After all, my visit was impromptu, to say the least. And I was guessing vampires didn't regularly hit the grocery store. Maybe he could call the pizza guy back? I could eat an entire pie at this point.

Logan gestured to the table, then walked over to the chair in front of the place setting, pulling it out. I sat down and he pushed it back in. Then he grabbed a napkin off the table and placed it in my lap with a flourish.

"What fine service," I couldn't help but quip.

A smile played at the corner of his mouth and I knew that my comment had pleased him. He walked out of the room, returning a moment later with a silver platter in his hands. He removed my plate and set the platter in front of me. Then he lifted the lid.

My mouth watered as the food was revealed. Roast chicken, swaddled in a medley of mini potatoes and colorful vegetables. Yes! Way better than some greasy old pizza. I had to force myself not to bury my face in the food I was so hungry. Instead, I casually picked up my fork.

"So, I assume you don't eat?" I asked, after taking my first bite and swallowing. The food was slightly cold, but extremely tasty. I grabbed the salt and sprinkled a little on top. Then I took a sip of the wine which turned out to be a very delicious petit Syrah.

"I can if necessary," he replied, sitting down next to me. Far too close for my liking. "But it makes me very sick to my stomach. I much prefer a liquid diet," he added, his mouth quirking.

"Right," I said, giving a brittle laugh. "So where is your paid blood donor then?"

He gave me a hard look. "Um, we're in hiding, remember? Not that I don't trust her to keep our secret. She's extremely loyal. But at the same time I wouldn't want to put her in a compromising situation. If they were to question her, I wouldn't want her to be forced to lie. Better she not know where I am for the moment."

"But how are you going to get your blood?" I blurted out. Then I bit my lower lip. "Not from me, I hope!"

He laughed. A deep, rich laugh. Then he reached over, brushing a lock of hair from my face. His touch sent chills spiraling to my toes and I could feel heat stain my cheeks. Damn it, why did this guy have such a hold on me? He barely touched me and I was completely on fire. More compulsion, perhaps? Cause this couldn't all be of my own free will.

"Trust me, sweetheart, your blood is safe," he assured me. "I can go a few days without drinking. It's not ideal, but it's not terrible either."

"If you say so," I muttered, taking another bite, followed by a large slug of wine. The formerly delicious food was now tasting like cardboard in my mouth. I was too distracted by the vampire sitting next to me. Watching me with his intense eyes. He had changed from earlier; the tux was gone. He was now wearing slouchy dark blue jeans, paired with a tight black t-shirt that stretched over his clearly perfect abs. Whoever heard of a vampire in jeans and t-shirt? I thought. But there was no doubt he pulled off the look marvelously.

I took another bite. Chewed. Swallowed. Glanced over at Logan who was still watching me with hungry eyes.

"What?" I asked, squirming a little my seat.

"I was just noticing how beautiful you are," he said simply.

I rolled my eyes. "And here I thought vampires had good eyesight. Was that another myth?"

To my surprise, he grabbed the chair. Jerked it around so I was suddenly facing him. As I gasped in surprise, he took my face in his cool, strong hands, forcing me to meet his eyes with my own. Such crazy eyes, I thought wildly, swirling with bits of blue and purple and green in a perfect storm. As if they couldn't make up their minds what color they should be and decided to fight it out.

"I have perfect eyesight," he said. "And you are goddamned beautiful. Whether you like it or not."

Holy crap. I didn't know what to say.

He laughed, tracing my jawline with a long finger. And suddenly I found myself hungry for something that was entirely not food. As Logan's hand dropped to my shoulder, skimming my collarbone, I felt myself begin to vibrate with want. With need. Against my better judgment I inched closer...

What are you doing? Stop this. Now!

My eyes flew open. I pushed backward in my chair with such force I almost knocked it over. Logan looked at me, a little dazed, as if he too had just awoken from a trance. I scrambled to my feet, backing away until I banged into the far wall of the dining room.

"I don't know what you think you're doing to me," I said, my voice trembling with a mixture of anger and fear. "But I'm not going to fall for it."

He cocked his head, looking genuinely confused. "What is it you think I'm doing to you?" he asked.

"Don't act all innocent. I know you have that compulsion thing. You used it on me to get me to come with you in the first place."

He nodded slowly. "We call it the vampire scent," he said quietly. "And yes, I did use it on you at the gala. To get you to come. I'm sorry about that—it wasn't very polite."

"No. It wasn't." I crossed my arms over my chest, scowling at him.

"But," he added. "I have not used it since. Any attraction you are feeling for me is all your own." A smile played at his lips, making my anger intensify. He was so sure of himself, wasn't he?

I glared at him. If looks could kill he would have been a puddle on the floor. He returned my look, as if daring me to try to take him on. At last I shook my head. Defeated.

"I need to use the restroom," I spit out. A ridiculous statement at a time like this, but I couldn't think of any more graceful way to bow out. And I couldn't just stay here, caught in his penetrating gaze for a moment longer.

He nodded. Gestured to the hall. "Third door to the right."

My face was burning now, as if on fire. I crossed the room.

Stepped into the hall. Everything inside me told me to run, but I couldn't give him the satisfaction. He loved it too much—this throwing me off balance. It amused him, even under our current dire circumstances. Which totally pissed me off.

I hardly think Miss Miller knows anything about vampires, he'd said at the book signing. *Or men for that matter.*

Shit. What was I doing? I was playing right into his hands. This was exactly what he wanted—what he'd asked for in the first place. For me to spend time with him, in his mansion. Was this whole thing just a ruse? Part of his elaborate show? Had the guy in the alleyway really tried to kill me? Or was the whole thing a setup by Logan? So he could roll in like a hero and save the day?

But you saw the guy go up in a puff of smoke, I reminded myself. *That couldn't have been faked.*

I reached the bathroom, stepping inside. Slamming the door behind me and locking it tight. Then I leaned against the wall, panting, trying frantically to catch my breath. This was all so totally crazy. Much too crazy. My heart was beating a mile a minute and my breath was coming in short gasps. For a moment I just stood there. Then I dropped to my knees as an unwanted desire rose up inside of me. My eyes locked on the cabinet drawers.

Biting my lower lip, I reached out, opening each drawer with bated breath, a prayer on my lips that it would contain what I was looking for. What I so desperately needed. Scissors. A nail file. Tweezers. A blade. Something—anything to cause a wound. To give myself some relief.

It was disgusting. Believe me, I knew it. Even as I pawed through hairbrushes and toothpastes, like a druggie searching for that elusive crack rock they just know they dropped in the carpet. Back home I had managed to make my habit seem almost sophisticated. A fancy blade in an even fancier box. It was a ritual. A tradition. At least that's what I liked to tell myself.

But any perceived glamour was gone now, all dignity stripped away as I wrapped my fingers around a small metal nail file, clutching it as if it were as precious as the Holy Grail. Not bothering to even shut the drawers, I climbed up onto the closed toilet seat, staring down at the piece of metal. Blood pounded in my ear. At the underside of my wrists. It was almost a rhythm, a song.

I glanced up at the bathroom door, tears streaming down my face. If only I could set the file down. If I could get up off this toilet seat. If I could walk away. Go out that door. Go back to dinner. Deal with things like a grown-up.

But in my heart I knew I was far too gone for that. I was too wound up. Too out of my element. I needed to get a handle on my emotions and this was the only way I knew how. And so, I sucked in a breath and determinedly dragged the file down my inner arm.

Of course a file isn't like a blade. It doesn't make that clean, perfect cut. I don't want to gross you out by going into too much detail, but it took a few tries before I achieved the desired result. That ribbon of red, slashing across my skin, that feeling of relief flooding my brain. I leaned back against the toilet, drawing in a deep breath. Allowing the endorphins to rush through my bloodstream. To calm my nerves.

It was all going to be okay. It was going to be totally—

There was a knock on the door. My eyes flew open.

"Hannah?" Logan's voice came from the other side. "Is everything all right? What's going on in there?"

Shit. I glanced down at my arm. I'd gotten a little too enthusiastic and it was bleeding more than I'd meant it to. I grabbed a swath of toilet paper and dabbed up the excess.

"Nothing!" I cried, my heart beating madly all over again. So much for my fleeting moment of relief. I glanced over to the closed door, trying to remember if I had locked it. Could Logan smell the blood from the other side? Like the vampire at the club had? He hadn't eaten—he had to be hungry. Would he be able to stop himself if he spotted the blood? "I just need a few more minutes," I added.

I looked down at my arm again. The blood had easily soaked through the thin toilet paper, turning it a dark crimson color. I grabbed more off the roll, trying to make it clot. God, I shouldn't have drunk that wine—it had probably thinned my blood, making it flow more freely.

The knock came again. Louder and more insistent this time. Then I saw the handle move, as if he was trying to turn it. Guess I had locked it after all.

"Open this door," Logan commanded in a voice that bordered on angry now. "Or I will break it down."

"Don't you dare!" I cried. "I'm fine! Just give me some fucking privacy, will you?"

Shit, shit, shit.

I looked around, desperate for something to stop the bleeding. The toilet paper was not cutting it. And the towels were all white, of course. Pristine and probably expensive. I shook my head. Screw it. After what he'd put me through I deserved a towel at the very least.

And so I grabbed a hand towel and wrapped it around my arm, moments before the door splintered. Logan burst into the bathroom, looking around, sniffing the air suspiciously. His eyes dropped to my arm, his pupils dilating. I let out a small squeak of fear and backed up against the wall. But, of course, there was nowhere to go. He was blocking the only exit.

"I...cut myself," I blurted out. "Stay away!"

He ignored me, stepping forward, invading my space. He grabbed my arm, unwrapping the towel. My heart beat furiously in my chest as I watched, trembling, wondering what he would do. My mind flashed back to the vampire outside the club again. How even the scent of my blood had practically driven him insane. And that had just been a small trickle...

For a moment, Logan just stared at the cut. Then, to my surprise, he gently lowered my arm. I watched as he walked over to the medicine cabinet and reached inside, pulling out a tube of Neosporin and a bandage. (Why hadn't I thought to look in there?)

"Apply this and then dress the wound," he said stiffly, handing both to me. "I can't take you to a doctor right now if it gets infected."

I stared at him, unable to speak. He wasn't going to drain me dry? I opened my mouth to say something, anything, but no words came out. He gave me a grim look, then stalked out of the bathroom, closing the splintered door behind him.

I let out a breath of relief. My mind flooding with awe at the scene that had just taken place. He'd never even lost control. Not for a second. Woodenly, I rose to my feet, dabbed the Neosporin on my cut and bandaged it up. Then I looked at myself in the mirror.

No more cutting, I told my reflection, all bloodshot eyes and sunken cheeks. I looked a mess. Completely zonked out of my skull. I looked down at my arm. At all the crisscrossed white scars—each one I had promised would be the last. Then my eyes went to the bandage and I firmed my resolve once more with feeling.

You're stronger than this, I told myself. *You don't need to do this.*

I glanced at the broken door. *You have no choice,* I added. *Otherwise next time you may not be so lucky.*

11

When I finally emerged from the bathroom, the dining room table had been cleaned off. All the delicious food was gone. My stomach panged with remorse. Next time I needed to eat before flipping the fuck out, I scolded myself.

I found Logan sitting in the parlor, reading a Tolstoy novel. He looked up when I entered the room and I was surprised to see the concern written on his handsome face. "Are you all right?" he asked, as if he really cared.

I felt my cheeks heat. Forcing myself to step into the room, I took a seat on one of the upholstered armchairs. "I'm fine," I said. "Sorry about that." I stared down at my lap, wringing my hands together. This was beyond embarrassing.

"Is that something you do often?" he asked in a soft voice.

I scowled, digging my nails into my palms. "I told you," I retorted. "I just cut myself. It's no big deal." I squirmed in my chair; if only I could sink into it and disappear.

His eyes zeroed in on me. "I see," he said. But I could tell he knew I was lying. Which only made the whole thing more embarrassing.

"It makes me feel better, okay?" I spit out, surprising even myself. "But I don't do it often. I mean, I used to do it a lot more. But I stopped. Well, I had stopped. But sometimes, when I get stressed..." I trailed off, my face on fire at this point.

For a moment, I stared down at my lap. Then, I slowly lifted my head, daring to meet Logan's gaze. I expected disgust. Maybe pity. But to my surprise there was none. Which only served to make me more upset.

"This is my fault!" I blurted out. "I did it in the alleyway. That's why the vampire attacked me. If I could have just had some goddamned self-control--"

"No."

I startled. Surprised at the force behind the word. "But--"

He shook his head. "No. It's not your fault. It's mine. I should have never taken you there. I don't know what I was thinking. It was just..." Now he was the one to look anguished. "I saw you in that bookstore. And I was so angry. To see you blithely taking people's money. Exploiting our kind. I hated you for doing that. I wanted you to see that this wasn't just a story to profit from. But real people's lives."

He rose to his feet, his hands clenching into fists. "But taking you there was wrong. I put you at risk. I had no right to do that." He scowled, slamming his fist against the wall. "And then... Well, I certainly should not have danced with you."

I bit my lower lip, my brain flooding back to that magical moment on the dance floor. Logan's hands circling my waist. His lips pressing against my own. The heat burning between our two bodies. The way my stomach had flopped like a fish out of water at his touch. I waited for the panic to rise inside of me all over again. But to my surprise, instead it was the heat that returned, low in my belly. I blushed again, but this time for a very different reason.

"I didn't mind the dancing," I admitted quietly. "It was kind of nice actually."

He gave a brittle laugh. "Then why did you run screaming for the exit?"

I snorted. "Let's just say... I don't get out much. And I certainly don't date. Not even humans."

He turned to face me. "Don't tell me no one asks you out."

"It's not that." I shook my head. "It's...a long story."

"And yet we've got nothing but time."

My heart thudded in my chest. Suddenly I wanted to tell him. Which was insane, crazy. I never talked about what happened to me that night. Not even to Darla. And the fact that I wanted to tell him—a practical stranger and a monster to boot—was terrifying. And didn't make any sense. I couldn't trust this guy. Not with my lunch order, never mind my most painful secret. Maybe he was using his compulsion again—that vampire scent. Trying to get me to show weakness. So he could gain the upper hand.

Well, that wasn't going to work on me. Not anymore.

"Enough about me. After all, aren't I here to learn about you?" I asked slyly, deftly changing the subject. "That was the whole reason you wanted me to come with you in the first place, right? So I could learn how to write real vampires?"

For a moment, he said nothing. Just looked at me with those piercing eyes of his. As if he could see into my very soul. Then he chuckled softly. "I suppose it was," he agreed. He settled back in his chair and set the book on a nearby table. "Very well, ask me what you will."

"How did you become a vampire?" I asked, figuring it was as good as any as a starting question. "Were you born or made?"

"No one is born a vampire. Vampirism is a disease. Someone has to give it to you."

"Who gave it to you? And how old are you anyway?"

"Thirty-five."

I raised an eyebrow. He laughed.

"You were expecting me to say a thousand, yes? Some vampires are that old. Many actually. But I was turned seven years ago. When I was twenty-eight years old." He smiled. "Thank God it wasn't when I was still a teenager like the vampires you see in the movies." He made a face. "Living through high school once was plenty, thank you very much."

I laughed. I couldn't help it. "Why do they do that, anyway?" I asked. "The whole vampire in high school thing? I mean, they could be out solving crimes or curing cancer or something. There has to be a better use of their eternal life than eternal high school."

"I don't think any real vampires attend high school," he assured me. Then his eyes twinkled. "And I've never seen any of them sparkle."

"Aw. That's actually kind of disappointing."

It was only then that I realized he hadn't answered the first part of my question. Who gave him vampirism? Maybe it was a sensitive subject. I decided not to bring it up again. At least for now.

"So if you're just a vampire newb, how come you were dressed like you stepped right off the pages of a Regency romance novel back at the bookstore?" I asked curiously. "You know, when you first came to my signing? Is *that* a vampire fashion thing? Like, for us, the nineties are back. For you it's the 1890s?"

He laughed. "I'd nearly forgotten about that. No. It's not a vampire thing. Definitely not. In fact, the last thing vampires want to do is stand out. To draw attention to themselves. Plus, those old fashioned clothes are so damn itchy." He grinned. "I was on my way to a birthday masquerade, as a matter of fact, and had only stopped by the bookstore to get a present for the birthday boy. You saw me in full on Mr. Darcy mode."

I nodded appreciatively. "Well, it was a good look on you," I teased. "Everyone thought you were my vampire hero."

He laughed, placing a hand to his chest. "*Did you ever know that you're my hero?*" he started singing, channeling his inner Bette Midler. "*And everything I would like to be!*"

I groaned, grabbing a nearby pillow and throwing it in his direction. He caught it and gave me a wicked grin. "See? Nineties kid. Through and through. Also, karaoke master."

I rolled my eyes. "*Anyway,*" I said. "Back to our Q and A. So what parts of the vampire mythos *did* Hollywood get right then?"

Logan seemed to consider this for a moment. "Most of it isn't far off," he said after a pause. "Holy water, churches, stakes— though they don't have to be made of wood to work. Cutting off a vampire's head also does the job. Though," he added. "I suppose cutting off anything's head would do the trick."

"Except zombies," I pointed out.

He grinned. "You don't seriously believe in zombies, do you?"

"Dude, after today I'm ready to believe in the Easter Bunny."

"Touché." He shifted in his seat. "In any case, as I mentioned before, we don't drink people dry. We have contracted blood donors. And we don't just randomly turn people into vampires either. We have a very specific vampire certification program each person has to go through before they are approved to become one of us."

"You have a vampire in training program?"

"Don't laugh! Remember, vampires live forever. We have to make sure each person is someone we can deal with for eternity."

"Hm. Good point." I thought about some of the people I'd

met over the years who I definitely didn't want to see achieve eternal life. Glad these vampires were picky.

"They're also given a partner," he added. "They call it a Blood Mate. They're the ones who turn the new vampires by sharing their blood and drinking some of their partner's. They bond together and spend eternity by one another's side." He shrugged. "Sort of like soul mates, but without actual souls."

"Do you have a blood mate?" I couldn't help but blurt out. Then I blushed. Was that like asking a vampire if he had a girlfriend?

He stared down at the ground and for a moment I thought he wouldn't answer. But finally he looked up. "I did," he said. "But she killed herself."

I stared at him. "What?"

"She was a thousand years old. She was sick of living, I guess. Bored of eternal life." He gave me a rueful look. "That's the number one killer of vampires, you know. Boredom. The world changing all around them, while they stay the same." He paused, then added, "That's why I took such objection to your character Jonathan. He's been around for two thousand years, right?"

"Close to that."

"And yet he has such a vibrant love for life. Such passion for Maisie. I don't know if I buy that."

"It's just a book. It's not supposed to be real."

He sighed loudly. "I know, I know. And I already apologized. I'll totally delete that one-star review."

I rolled my eyes. "Yeah, yeah. So you keep saying."

"How did you become a vampire writer anyway?" he asked. "Did you actually grow up liking them? Or was it just because of that dream you mentioned?"

"A little of both," I admitted. "My Mom was a total goth girl and was always taking me to vampire movies and such. But that dream! I mean it was like Jonathan literally came to me. Fully formed. As if he were real and asked me to write his story."

"So you are legit *Interview with a Vampire*," Logan teased.

I rolled my eyes. "Yeah, yeah." I shook my head. "Anyway, I started writing. And I put the first book up online to see how it would do. I expected to make like ten bucks. Instead, I made close to ten million."

Logan gave a low whistle. "People really want to read about vampires that badly?"

"Evidently so. My readers are truly--"

But I never got a chance to finish the sentence. A crash interrupted me, followed by the sound of shattering glass. I glanced over at Logan, my heart in my throat. He was already on his feet. A moment later an alarm began to wail.

"They must have found us somehow," he said in a low voice. "We need to get out of here. Now."

12

I somehow managed a nod, glancing nervously at the door. But Logan, it seemed, had other plans. He pulled up a rug, revealing a trapdoor.

"You have a real life secret passage?" I couldn't help but ask. Man, this house really did have everything, didn't it?

He didn't answer, concentrating on lifting up the door, which revealed a dark pit—and a ladder leading into nothingness. I swallowed hard. I hated closed-in spaces. But the shouts of the intruders were getting closer and it seemed this was our only option of escape. I would have to find a way to deal.

"We have the place surrounded," one of them yelled, as if to prove my point. "Come out now, or we will come and get you ourselves."

Logan motioned for me to go first. Of course. Sucking in a breath, I forced my feet to obey, my entire body shaking with fear. My hands wrapped around the rungs of the ladder as I started down, step by step, until I was completely engulfed in blackness. I gritted my teeth; did no one ever think of installing a light switch in their secret tunnel? Would that have been so damn hard?

I could hear Logan above and tried to concentrate on the sound of his own feet, hitting each rung as he followed me down. Reminding myself that at least I wasn't alone.

But that thought wasn't nearly comforting enough once Logan pulled the rug back over the trap door and closed it behind us, eclipsing the small sliver of light from above. Now we were in total cave darkness and I had to bite down on my lower lip, so as not to whimper with fear.

I would have made a very crappy book heroine. But you try being brave at a time like this. See how you do!

Down and down I went. How deep was this pit anyway? Would it really bring us somewhere safe? *Was* there anywhere safe anymore?

Finally, after what seemed an eternity, I felt my feet connect with the floor. I dropped down, practically moaning in relief at the feeling of solid ground beneath me. A moment later, I felt Logan step down next to me. He reached out, finding my hand and taking it into his own. I let out a breath I didn't realize I was holding.

"Tell me you didn't forget the flashlight," I managed to squeak.

His warm laugh rippled through the air. "Don't worry, little writer. I can see just fine down here."

Okay then. Vampire night vision. Check. One more fun fact for the day.

And so I had no choice but to let him lead, down the blackened passageway, so dark I couldn't see my hand in front of my face. My other hand was having a much better time of things, locked in Logan's own. His grip was strong, yet gentle. Cool in temperature, but warm in intention. As if to assure me he had things under control. That he wouldn't let anything happen to me. Not under his watch.

It shouldn't have made me feel better, but somehow it did.

We walked for what felt like forever, but was probably only ten minutes or so. When we finally stopped, I heard something —the scrape of a lock? A moment later a sliver of light appeared. A door was opening. I let out a breath of relief as Logan ushered me inside. Thank God. No more darkness.

We emerged into a luxurious looking hallway, walls covered with paintings from famous artists that didn't look like replicas. Logan closed the door behind us then turned to me, his eyes piercing down at me, assessing my well-being.

"Are you all right?" he asked.

I managed a nod. "Who were those people?" I asked. "Other vampires?"

"I believe they were from Slayer, Inc.," he replied.

I winced, remembering him talking about Slayer, Inc. earlier. If they were really after us...

"But you were only protecting me!" I protested, even as guilt swam through my stomach. No matter what Logan said, I knew this was my fault. And now they had a hit out on him, because he had saved my sorry ass.

"Right. Well, that's what I'm going to try to explain when I plead my case," he replied. "While the life of a mortal doesn't hold as much value to the Consortium than that of a vampire's, there's still a strict code against attacking humans."

I pursed my lips. His argument sounded weak at best. I sure hope it worked. I looked around. "Where are we, anyway?" I asked.

"The Blood Coven headquarters."

"What?" My heart started beating fast again. We were in a *vampire* coven? An actual, legit, underground *vampire* coven? Talk about going from the frying pan to the fire. "But won't they turn us in if they find us here?"

"I am going to talk to the Master," Logan explained. "Jareth is a good man. If anyone will understand, he will."

The hallway dead-ended at a wooden door, guarded by two men. Two vampires, to be precise. When they saw me, they gave me a disapproving once over, their eyes raking from my head to my toes. As if I were gum they had discovered on the bottoms of their shoes.

They turned to Logan. "What is it?" the first one asked. "The Master is very busy."

Logan returned their look. "He won't be too busy for me."

The guards exchanged glances, then shrugged. The second one turned to open the door behind him. "Wait here," he said, before slipping through and closing it again. I glanced at Logan, my body still humming with nerves. He gave me a sympathetic smile and reached out to squeeze my hand.

Gah! His cool, strong touch sent spirals of feels spinning out to every extremity. Seriously, what was it about this guy that made my body sing like a canary, every time he came close? Was it the vampire scent thing? But no, the guard standing in front of me was also a vampire. And he was doing nothing for me. Nor had the guy outside the club—even before he attempted to drain me dry.

It was Logan and Logan alone who got my engines purring. And that could turn out, I realized, to be a huge problem.

I started to pull my hand away. But at that moment the guard returned. He ushered Logan through the door. "You stay here," he said to me in a curt voice. "No humans allowed beyond this point."

I glanced down the empty hall, my nerves returning with a vengeance. "Here?" I asked. I shot a pleading look at Logan. I didn't want to be left alone. Not with Slayer Inc on our tails.

"At least let her come into the waiting room," he said to the guard.

The vampire didn't look happy, but widened the door and allowed me in.

We stepped into a plush waiting room, all decked out in velvet and crimson. These vampires really did like the whole Victorian-chic thing. Once inside, I obediently sat myself down on one of the sofas and grabbed a magazine. It was a tabloid, funny enough. Race Jameson the rock star was on the cover. Wait, was he a vampire? That would explain a LOT.

I looked up, realizing Logan was still staring at me, a concerned expression on his face. "Go, do your vampire thing," I told him. "I'm good here."

He looked relieved and turned back to the guard who led him into the inner chamber, where evidently the big bad vampire master was. I watched them go, preparing to turn back to my magazine and read the Race Jameson story—I'd always been a big fan. But before I could, a teenage girl danced out the door the vampires had just exited from. She stopped when she saw me, raising an eyebrow.

"What are *you* doing here?" she asked.

I stared at her. She had dyed, black shoulder-length hair, pale skin, red lips. She was wearing this lacy black dress paired with heavy looking combat boots. But it wasn't her outfit that threw me the most. It was how familiar she looked.

"You're...?" I racked my brain trying to place her.

"Rayne McDonald," she said. Then her mouth broke out into a huge smile. "I'm your biggest fan!"

Wait, what?

And then it hit me. Exactly where I knew this girl from. She was a member of my online street team. Darla had suggested I do a street team after the first book went crazy. I called them the Amazing Maisies. And they helped me spread the word during book releases, in exchange for advanced copies of the books and other swag.

What on earth was a member of my street team doing down here? And why was she walking out of the coven master's inner sanctum, as if she owned the place? Was she one of those blood donors Logan spoke about? Or...

She plopped herself down beside me, her eyes shining with enthusiasm. "Oh my God, it's such an honor to meet you," she gushed. "Your books. They are life-changers. I've read every single one of them at least three times. The way you describe vampires!" She pretended to swoon. "If only they were like that in real life."

I frowned. What was it with people telling me my characters weren't like real vampires? Though I supposed they weren't entirely wrong, from what I'd seen so far. Still, couldn't they just leave me a one-star review somewhere? Did they have to keep rubbing it in my face?

"It's...uh, nice to meet you, too," I stammered, feeling as if she expected me to say something. "Do you...are you...?" Okay, so my mouth wasn't working too well. But do you blame me?

She grinned. "Yes. I'm a vampire. I'm also a fairy. And I'm on the cheerleading squad."

"Cheerleading?" I looked her in disbelief, then blushed. Because duh, that was like the least weird thing she had just said.

"It's a long story." She smiled at me. "What are you doing here? Are you doing research for your books? Do you need a model for your new characters? Just say the word—I'm your vampire!"

"It's a little more serious than that, I'm afraid," I said, staring down at my hands. I told her about the vampire at the club. About Logan taking me back home. About Slayer Inc.

"What?" Rayne cried indignantly when I mention the vampire slaying organization. "How dare they threaten my favorite author! I am going to have a word with T-Dogg."

"T-Dogg?"

"Oh, Mr. Teifert. He's the Slayer Inc. Vice President. Also, the drama teacher at my old high school. Super nice guy, actually. At least when he doesn't hold a commission to kill you."

"I'm sure he's...lovely."

She rose to her feet. "Don't worry. I've got this." She headed to the door. "No way I'm letting anyone slay *you*. At least not until you finish your series."

I gave her a weak smile, suddenly reminded of a certain Stephen King book. "That's...um...very kind of you....Um..."

"Rayne," she reminded me. Then she reached into her pocket and pulled out a piece of paper. "Here's my cell. Call me if you need anything. Anything at all."

I took it from her, still feeling completely baffled by the scene. "Thank you," I said. "I really appreciate it."

"No problem." She paused, then added. "Oh, but I do have one request."

I raised an eyebrow.

"Can Jade *please* get her own story someday? And her own vampire? It's so not fair having the sister be nothing more than a sidekick with a great sense of humor."

I laughed. "You definitely are not the first reader to ask that."

"But I'm the reader who's saving your life," she shot back, not missing a beat. "So, you know. Turn around, fair play, all that?"

"I'll consider it."

Rayne gave me one last smile, then danced out of the room. I watched her go, shaking my head. Who would have thought I'd find a fan down here? It really was a strange world.

The door opened then. Logan stepped out, a troubled look on his face. I rose to my feet. "Is everything okay?" I asked.

He shrugged. "It's fine," he said, though his expression said otherwise. He forced a smile to his face. "Jareth said we could stay here for a bit. Where we'll be safe."

"Great," I said. And I was surprised to realize I actually meant it. Before tonight I would have been horrified at the idea of sleeping in an underground crypt filled with real life vampires. But it had been a long 24 hours.

A porter showed up, seemingly out of nowhere. "I'll take you to your room," he said.

I frowned. "He means rooms, right?" I hissed at Logan. He shot me a warning look, but didn't reply.

We walked down an ornate hallway with dark carpet and oil portraits on the wall, alternating with dim sconces. I tried to take in every detail—maybe I could use this place in one of my books someday. If I got out of this mess in the end.

The porter stopped in front of a nondescript door that looked, to me anyway, exactly the same as every other door we'd passed in the hall. He reached into his pocket and pulled out a long, silver key. No card locks at Hotel Transylvania evidently. I suddenly wondered if they had Wi-Fi. I still hadn't emailed Darla. She must be freaking out hardcore at this point.

The door creaked open. Logan gestured for me to step inside. I did, finding the equivalent of a hotel room. A king sized bed. A dresser. An armchair. No windows, of course. But no coffins either. So there was that.

"Is this my room?" I asked.

The porter looked confused. "It's for the two of you," he said. "You are betrothed, are you not?"

"Betrothed?" I coughed out.

Logan stamped on my foot. Then he put a loving arm around me and smiled at the porter. "This is perfect," he said, handing him a wad of bills. "Thank you."

The porter shrugged. "Do you need ice?"

"We'll be fine. Just...call me when my donor arrives."

The porter nodded, as if this was a perfectly natural request. Blood room service. Why not? He stepped out of the room, shutting the door behind him.

Leaving me once again alone with a vampire.

13

I waited to hear the porter's footsteps fade. Then I turned to face Logan, hands on my hips. "Betrothed?" I spit out. "What the hell?"

He gave me a withering look. "I had no choice," he said. "Bringing a mortal down to the Blood Coven sanctuary is already forbidden. A mortal who is wanted by Slayer Inc.? That's even worse." He walked over to the nearby chair, sinking down onto it. He was so tall, he barely fit.

"So you told them we were engaged," I concluded.

"Yes. It is acceptable, though not exactly encouraged, for vampires to get married to mortals when they're younger," he said. "It's only later, when they close in on the thousand-year mark that they are required to take a Blood Mate and leave mortal life behind for good."

"I see."

"Don't worry," he said dryly. "Your honor will remain intact. I'll sleep in the chair. You can take the bed."

I frowned, giving him a once-over. "You barely fit in that chair. There's no way you'll be able to sleep in it."

"I've slept in worse."

I glanced at the bed. It did look cozy. And I was exhausted at this point. I knew the second my head hit the pillow I'd pass out. Also, if Logan had been interested in taking my honor, or however he put it, he had had many chances already. It would seem unlikely he'd pick now for my vampire deflowering.

"This is ridiculous," I said. "It's a huge bed. We can share it."

He gave me a doubtful look. "I don't want to make you feel uncomfortable."

"Dude, we've passed uncomfortable miles ago. I'll make it work."

To prove my point, I kicked off my shoes and crawled into the bed, sticking my feet under the covers. The sheets felt silky against my aching skin. Clearly high thread count. I needed to check to see what brand they were before I left.

I turned to Logan, patting the side of the bed. He eyed it for a moment, then joined me, also taking off his shoes. He didn't go under the covers though. I had to admit, he was pretty honorable for a thirty-five-year-old. Maybe some of those more Victorian vampire manners had worn off on him.

I felt something flutter in my chest. He really was a nice guy. I had totally misjudged him back at my book signing and then again at the charity ball. He'd seemed so aggressive back then. As if he was used to just taking what he wanted. Now I was seeing a different side of him. And honestly, it felt more genuine. As if this was his true self. The self he didn't want the world to see. And I kind of liked it.

I raked my gaze down his body. I kind of liked him in my bed, too, if we were being honest here. Which was crazy, to say the least. I, Hannah, did not do guys in my bed. But, hey, maybe I was having of change of heart, too. I felt a warm feeling rise in my throat.

"So what did Jareth say?" I asked, pushing it back down.

After all, Logan had basically just promised not to jump me. Which likely meant he didn't want to be jumped *by* me either.

"Just...that he'd do what he could," Logan replied, getting that uncomfortable look on his face again.

I frowned. "You don't sound too optimistic."

"Eh." He waved me off. "I'm sure it will all work out. In any case I made it very clear to Jareth that you should not have been involved in any of it. That you were an innocent party—attacked without provocation. No matter what ends up happening to me, I made sure you will be able to go free. Get back to your old life."

I nodded slowly, knowing the words should be meaning more to me than they were. I should be happy—thrilled—to know that this could all just go away. I could get back to reality. My apartment, my books. Darla and my cat. Leave all this supernatural stuff behind. But then...

"What about you?" I blurted out.

For a moment he said nothing. Then he sighed. "There will be a trial, I'm sure," he said. "I'll hire a lawyer. Try to make my case. Find some character witnesses..." He shrugged. "I have a lot of friends in the vampire community. And a spotless record. Surely they will take that under consideration."

But something in his eyes told me that he wasn't sure at all. Which made something painful tug hard at my chest. Instinctively, I reached out, slipping my hand into his. "I'm sorry," I said for the millionth time.

Logan squeezed my hand. He had such strong fingers, and yet so gentle at the same time. He turned to look at me, his eyes meeting mine. He looked so sad. It tore at my heart. When he reached up to brush a lock of hair out of my eyes something inside of me melted.

"Oh Hannah," he said. "I wanted so badly to show you how vampires lived. I'm afraid I haven't given you much to work with."

I forced a small smile, my heart pounding in my chest. Our faces were inches apart. Our hands entwined. Suddenly I felt brave.

"You still have time," I said slowly, letting the words drag out. Then I tilted my head, ever so slightly toward him. It was a small move, barely noticeable. But for me it might as well have been moving mountains. Giving an invitation I had so long withheld from any guy.

For a moment he just looked at me. As if he couldn't believe what I was offering. But I held his gaze, assuring him it was what I wanted. And so he reached up, taking my head in his hands and pulling me toward him until our mouths were on one another's. Our tongues entwined in a wild dance that sent shivers to my toes. My mind spun. Nerve endings tickling my every extremity.

Oh God. This was happening This was really happening.

I groaned as I moved against him, suddenly lost in a world of lust and desire I hadn't felt in years. His hands dropped to my shoulders, then to my waist, dragging me closer until I was flush against him. My breasts squashed against his solid chest. Our legs wrapped in a complicated puzzle. He tasted so good. He felt so good. And it had been so long. So, so long since--

His hand dragged up my ribcage, his thumb grazing the tip of my breast. I gasped as the sensation struck me like a lightning strike.

Then, something in my brain spiked. And horrifying visions rocked through my synapses.

Rough hands. Grabbing at my flesh. Ignoring my pleas. Ignoring my sobs.

Somehow my hands found Logan's chest and I shoved him backward with all my might. Then I lunged off the bed, so fast I almost fell on the floor. Instead, I stumbled to the back side of the room, by the door, sinking to the ground, hugging my knees in my hands. Tears fell from my eyes like rain, staining my shirt.

Logan stared at me for a moment. A dazed look on his face. Then he rose from the bed. Walked over to me.

"Don't touch me!" I cried. "Please don't touch me!"

To his credit, he didn't try. Even though he looked as if he wanted to desperately. And not in a sexual way either. But as if he just wanted to hold me. To comfort me.

And a huge part of me wanted him to do just that. To have him wrap those strong arms around me. To have him whisper in my ear that everything would be okay. But that would just lead to more of what had just happened. What couldn't happen again.

God. I buried my face in my lap. I felt like such a fool. What was I thinking? That I was some normal girl with a normal guy who could just enjoy stuff normal people enjoyed?

Logan walked to the opposite side of the room. Sank down into that damn miniature chair again. I waited for him to say something. Anything. But he didn't. Which was really nice of him, actually. Most people would have demanded answers. What the hell was that all about? Why was I acting so crazy? Why was I such a tease?

But Logan was not like most people. Of that, I was certain.

I sucked in a breath, my face flushed with how ridiculous my actions must seem to him. After all, this was not a dark alleyway. I hadn't been in any danger. I didn't think for a moment that Logan wouldn't have listened to me if I asked him nicely to stop.

And yet I had, once again, totally freaked out. Pushed myself away from a guy. Was I doomed to this pattern for the rest of my life? Would I ever be a real woman again? A woman with the capacity to share herself with a guy? Or had I let that monster rob me of that, too?

The urge to cut came sharp as a blade. I stared down at the

white crosses on my left arm. The bandage still on my right. There was probably a scab. I could pick the scab...

"That's not a good idea," Logan said. "Not here."

My head jerked up. "What isn't?" I asked, my heart pounding in my chest all over again. I felt like I was going to be sick.

He nodded in the direction of my arm. My face burned with shame.

"Did you read my thoughts?" I demanded, rising to my feet.

He shook his head. "I can't read thoughts," he said. "Some vampires can. I can't."

I glanced down at my arm. "Then how...?"

"Simple. I see your past, written on your arms. I know what you did in my bathroom. And I know you want to do it here." He gave me a rueful look. "But that would be a very bad mistake. There are a lot of vampires here tonight. They would break down that door to get to you if they smelled even a hint of your blood. And then I'd have to kill them all. Which," he added with a small quirk at his mouth. "Wouldn't exactly help my case."

I groaned, leaning back against the wall. Could I be any more embarrassed than I was at this very moment? "I'm sorry," I said. "I'm so sorry."

"You don't have anything to apologize for." He gave me a sympathetic look. "I'm the one who should be sorry. I made you feel uncomfortable."

I thought back to the scene on the bed. "You made me feel good," I said. "Just...maybe a little too good." I blushed again. "I don't...do that kind of thing. Not with anyone."

"Why not?"

It was such a simple question. But with such a complicated answer. "It's a long story."

He glanced at his watch. "We've got all day."

He was right, of course. We weren't going anywhere. But that didn't mean I wanted to spend the time spilling my heart to a practical stranger.

But *was* he a stranger? Something inside me niggled. He was starting not to feel that way. Sure, we hadn't known each other long. But the intensity of our brief relationship had fast tracked us to a strange sense of intimacy of a friendship that was far longer.

I didn't have a lot of people I trusted these days. I lost most of my so-called friends after that night. When they stuck up for him instead of me. When they said I should just let it go. Not make it a big deal. That I shouldn't ruin someone's entire life because of one drunken mistake.

Sure, I had Darla. But Darla was so innocent. So sweet and happy. I never wanted to drag her down with my darkness.

But now, here I was, sitting in a room with darkness himself. And for some weird reason I felt compelled to tell him everything. Let him hear it all. Every last dirty detail. And learn, once and for all, if he was just like the rest of them.

"I was raped," I blurted out. Because that's what it was. Why beat around the bush? You could call it date rape. Somehow that seemed to soften it in people's minds. As if that was somehow better. That someone you knew and trusted did those things to you. The line of consent blurring. Had you been kissing? Had you worn a short skirt? Had you teased him all night, batting your eyes?

Such a slut.

Totally asked for it.

He'd had such a great future ahead of him. So much to look forward to.

And then she...ruined his life.

It would have been so much better had it been a stranger. Some random face I could push out of my head and never think of again. A violent act I could condemn utterly and know was not my fault whatsoever.

But raped by your own boyfriend? That was a slippery slope.

"I'd been seeing this guy for a couple months," I said. "Casually. We were both super busy in school—he was studying to be a politician. His dad was—*is* a state senator. But whenever we had free time we'd go out. He was pretty nice—or so I thought. Charming, handsome, popular. You know the type."

A shadow seemed to cross Logan's face. But, "Yes," was all he said.

"Anyway, he invited me to this house party. In some big mansion off campus that one of his friends' parents' owned. It was supposed to be the party of the semester. I was pretty excited to get an invite." I snorted. "Let's just say I wasn't the most popular girl in school, even then.

"Honestly, the whole thing was one big walking cliché. I got there. I started drinking. Everyone was drinking. I mean, it was a college party, duh. I remember dancing out by the pool. Having a great time. And then...things sort of got fuzzy around the edges. I guess I passed out."

My heart started beating a little faster as my mind revisited the scene. I wondered if I should stop talking. Surely he could fill in the blanks. It was a tale as old as time, after all.

"Go on," he said.

I closed my eyes, biting my lower lip for a moment before continuing. "I woke up in a bed. My underwear was at my ankles. There was someone on top of me—it was dark, I couldn't see who it was at first. I cried out, trying to get him to stop. To leave me alone. But my head was still so fuzzy. My tongue so thick—it wasn't working right. He pressed a hand to my mouth to stop me from screaming. He leaned down and whispered in my ear." I swallowed hard. "That's when I realized who it was."

"Your boyfriend," Logan concluded. Not looking happy.

I nodded, staring down at the floor, no longer able to look at him. "I let him finish. I didn't say anything else. I probably should have fought harder. But at the time I didn't know if I had the strength. And what did it matter at that point anyway? He was already halfway done. I thought—if I could just suck it up. Get through it somehow, it'd be over. And then I could pretend it never happened."

"Oh Hannah," Logan's voice was filled with pity, warring with fury.

I waved him off. I had to finish. I'd gone too far to stop now. "When he was done, he rolled over and basically passed out. I tried to sleep, too. But my heart was racing. Finally, I got up. I staggered out of the bedroom. People were staring at me as I walked through the living room. I could hear them giggling. Whispering. Not surprising, I suppose. I must have looked a sight. I walked straight out the front door, not even bothering to find my shoes. Walked four miles to get home."

"You didn't go to the police?"

I hung my head. "I did actually. Well, sort of. Once I got home my mother took one look at me and dragged me to the hospital. They did an examination. Found out I'd been roofied. I begged them not to call the cops, but it was a crime; they had to report it." I made a face. "The next day it was all over school. Jake had been arrested. Suspended, too. And kicked off the football team. That was probably the worst part. He was their star player. In their minds I had lost the season for them."

Such a slut.

Totally asked for it.

Then...ruined his life.

The tears welled in my eyes as my mind relived those horrible weeks that followed. The weeks that would haunt me forever.

"The good thing was, it sort of killed my social life," I said, giving him a rueful smile. "Which made me start writing." I shrugged. "The rest is history, I guess."

Logan rose from the chair. Walked over to the bed. For a moment he just looked down at me. His eyes rimmed with red. Then he dropped to his knees, opening his arms. Inviting, but not insisting. Which made my heart swell.

I threw myself into his embrace. An embrace that was so strong, it was almost crushing—yet felt so good at the same time. Solid, real, infused with strength. My muscles relaxed. My body melting into his. I pressed my face against his chest, breathing in his warm, comfortable scent. He smelled like the forest. A wild, dark forest. Dangerous, yet at the same time, so safe. As if nothing bad could possibly happen when locked in his arms. And as he stroked my hair, his fingernails lightly scraping against my scalp, I felt more at peace than I could remember feeling for ages. Maybe ever.

"Is it wrong that I want to kill him?" Logan whispered in my ear, his voice husky and angry in a way that sent chills down my spine. "Drain every last drop of blood from his body?"

I found myself smiling against him. "You'd drain someone dry for me?"

"Sweetheart, I'd rip them from limb to limb."

The fierceness in his voice sent chills winding through me again. I sucked in a shaky breath, my insides flip-flopping like a fish out of water. I thought about his words back at that book signing. How I didn't know how to write real men. And maybe he was right. I certainly never wrote anyone like him.

I pulled away from our embrace. Until I met his eyes with my own. They were filled with such a strange mixture of fury and admiration. My mouth parted. My heart pounded in my chest. I found myself leaning forward. My fear evaporating. Replaced by the nearly overwhelming desire to taste him again.

But before I could, he placed a finger to my lips. I watched as he slowly shook his head.

"No," he said.

"What?" I stared at him, confused. "What do you mean, no?" I demanded, frustration spilling over. "I thought this was what you wanted."

He gave me an agonized look. "Believe me, I want nothing more in the entire world than to kiss you right now. But I won't do it."

"I don't understand." My mind raced, suddenly panicked. "Is it because of what I told you? Do you think I'm...dirty or something?" I bit my lower lip. "Used?"

He looked horrified. "No!" he cried. "That never crossed my mind!" He pulled me to him, sitting me on his lap. He reached out, stroking my cheek with a gentle hand. I knew he could crush me with little effort. And yet, he was so gentle. So fucking gentle. As if I were a doll he was afraid to break.

"Sweetheart, you have been through so much. And to rush you into something else—before you are ready? I would be as bad as him. I will not take advantage of you. I will not take what you're not ready to give. I will wait until you are truly ready." He paused, a small smile crossing his face. "After all, vampires have all the time in the world."

My heart squeezed. The emotions driving through me now, too hard and fast to catalog. The words he spoke, the consideration he gave. The fact that he cared enough, respected me enough. It was almost too much to bear.

"Come," he said, gesturing to the bed. He pulled back the covers, revealing crisp, white sheets. I reluctantly crawled under the blanket. He replaced it over me.

Then he leaned down, kissing my forehead. Such a light kiss, I should have barely felt it. Yet it burned against my skin as if it had set me on fire. I looked up at him, affection streaming through me. Gratitude making it difficult to speak.

"Thank you," I said at last. It sounded so lame coming from my lips, but I didn't know what else to say.

He smiled. Then he walked around the bed and sank into the chair again. Closed his eyes. I watched him for a moment, taking him in. Wondering what he was thinking. What he thought of me. Then I snuggled under the covers, pulling my knees to my chest. Trying to get comfortable. Trying to still my fast-beating heart.

I had just settled in when there was a crisp knock on the door. I opened my eyes, my heart pounding all over again. I glanced over at Logan who had risen from his chair and was walking across the room. He gave me an apologetic glance.

"Sorry," he said. "I think it's my donor. I forgot she was coming."

I sat up in bed, pulling the covers to my chin. Logan opened the door, revealing a young girl with long black hair that tumbled down her back in waves. She was beautiful, voluptuous, and wearing a skin-tight black dress that accentuated every curve of her body and every swell of her envious breasts. Wow. Logan had said he used a blood donor. He didn't say she was a raven haired Marilyn Monroe.

"There you are, handsome," she purred, stepping into the room. I watched as she reached out, dragging a well-manicured fingernail down Logan's chest. "How long has it been?" she added. "Poor boy. You must be simply starving!"

Logan let out a low growl, deep in his throat. Almost feral in its intensity. His eyes locked onto her body, giving her a greedy look. He stepped forward, then stopped short. Seeming to remember he and his little blood chick weren't alone. He glanced back at me.

"Sorry," I stammered, feeling suddenly like an interloper. "Should I get out of your way?"

He pursed his lips. Then he shook his head. "No," he said. "You stay and get some sleep. We can do this elsewhere."

I watched as he put a possessive arm around the girl, leading her out of the room. She smiled up at him, as if they shared some kind of secret—just between the two of them. When they closed the door behind them, I collapsed back onto the bed, staring up at the ceiling, my heart wrenching in my chest. Trying not to imagine them alone together. His lips on her neck. Her soft mews as his fangs sank into her willing flesh.

While I lay here alone.

I felt the tears slip from the corners of my eyes. I rolled over to my side, again pulling my knees to my chest. Trying to hug away the sudden intense feeling of loneliness. The helplessness that rose through me like a tidal wave. I thought back to our encounter just a few moments before. When the lust in his eyes had been focused on me. He'd wanted me. He was ready to take me. But I had refused him—turned him away. Who was I now to feel bad about him going to someone else? Someone who wouldn't make him feel like a jerk.

"She's just dinner," I told myself. "She doesn't mean anything to him."

But, of course, that wasn't true. Of course she meant something to him. After all, she could give him something. Something he wanted. Something he needed.

Unlike little old me. Unable to give anything at all.

14

I woke up sometime later to find Logan sitting in the chair, reading something on his phone. Stretching my arms over my head, I released a long yawn. I couldn't believe how great I had slept, considering the place and circumstances. I should have been tossing and turning in fear. Instead, I'd conked out like a baby.

Logan looked up from his phone. He gave me a slow smile. "You're awake," he said.

"I guess so." I sat up in bed, brushing my hair back from my shoulder. "God, I slept like the dead."

"It's the being underground," he explained. "There's no light. There's no sound. It's very conducive to sleep."

"What about you? I mean, that chair couldn't have been comfortable," I said, giving him a sheepish look. In the light of day the whole thing seemed so ridiculous. So embarrassing. I couldn't believe I had led him on like that, then yanked away. He must think I was a total freak.

But his smile never wavered. "It was fine," he assured me, stretching his arms and legs, as if to prove his point. Instead he almost fell off the chair. He laughed and stood up. "Okay, I admit. It wasn't the most comfortable sleep I've ever had. But it's all good."

I groaned, throwing myself back on the pillow. "Seriously, I am the worst damsel in distress ever," I said.

"I don't know about that," he shot back. "And at least you're a damn good kisser."

Oh. My. God.

My face flamed. I grabbed the pillow and pulled it over my head. Logan laughed and grabbed it from me. I tried to wrestle it back, but, of course he was too strong. Cause, you know. Vampire.

But I wasn't about to be thwarted. I grabbed the other pillow and threw it in his direction. It him square in the chest. He waggled his eyebrows at me.

"Oh I see," he said. Then he grabbed both pillows and charged me. I ducked, but it was no use. I was hit with both of them square on.

"Uncle!" I protested as he jumped onto the bed. "Uncle!"

He laughed, but dropped the pillows. Then he lay, out of breath, on the bed, staring up at the ceiling, I lay next to him, so close we were almost touching, yet frustratingly still inches apart. I knew it wouldn't take much to make that move. To cross that boundary again. To climb on top of him, straddle his thighs. To lean down and kiss him senseless.

But then what? What if my anxiety returned? I couldn't lead him on, then push him away a second time. That would just be cruel. And what if he decided he'd had enough of me? That I wasn't worth his time or attention?

No. It was better to wait. At least until I felt more comfortable. Till I got control of my senses. And maybe until we were out of danger. Now there was a thought. It was tough to remember, actually, that we were technically still on the run. Still in fear of our lives. This bedroom felt like the perfect hideaway. As if there was no one left in the world outside.

"Are you okay?" he asked, leaning over and propping his body up on his elbow. He reached out, tracing my cheek with a careful finger. It was such a simple gesture. And yet done with such tenderness. My heart squeezed.

"I'm fine," I said. "I mean, as fine as I can be, under the circumstances."

His face sobered. "Yeah," he said. "Again, I'm so sorry."

I reached out, pressing a finger to his lips this time. "No more apologies," I scolded. "I wasn't exactly an innocent party to all of this either. I refuse to let you take all the blame."

"You're sweet," he said. "But I must insist on all of the blame." His mouth quirked. "That's how I roll."

I burst out laughing. I couldn't help it. "You know, I keep expecting you to say all these weird old vampire things," I said. "And I keep forgetting you're like the only vampire who's not a thousand years old."

"There are plenty of younger vampires," he assured me. "Like your little fan Rayne MacDonald. She's only about ten vampire years old."

"So...that makes her, what? Like twenty-six? Twenty-seven? She looks like a teenager."

"She was turned as a teen. She had a terrible virus and was going to die. And so Jareth made her his Blood Mate."

"Aw. That's pretty romantic actually," I said with a dreamy sigh. "Just like in one of my novels."

To my surprise Logan said nothing. When I glanced over at him I saw the playful look had vanished from his face.

It was then that I remembered what he'd said about his own Blood Mate back at his house. How she'd killed herself, bored with life. I suddenly wondered if there was more to it than that.

What had their relationship been like when she was still

alive? Had she been more to him than simply a blood surrogate? Had they been together at one point? Blood Mates, lovers, husband and wife? Was he devastated when she took her own life? Did he still hold out feelings for her?

"So...your Blood Mate..." I started, suddenly feeling desperate to know. "Was she—"

Logan jerked from the bed. Stalked to the end of the room. The one that, if this were a hotel, would have had been lined with windows. But since we were underground he had to stare at a blank wall.

Okay, then. Guess we wouldn't be talking about that.

"Sorry," I said, walking over to him. Feeling brave, I reached out and took his hand in mine, squeezing it a little. "I didn't mean to pry."

He turned to me, his expression anguished. "No. I'm the one who's sorry," he said. "It's just..." He sighed. "Let's just say you're not the only one with a painful past."

I gave him a rueful smile, my heart swelling with affection, mixed with sorrow. It was so strange to look at him now. To see the same big, bad vampire who had come off as such an arrogant asshole when I first met him. Now I saw there was so much more to him. A depth and sadness he'd been desperately trying to hide.

I wanted to ask a billion questions. But I realized I wanted him to be ready to answer when I did. After all, I knew all too well what it was like to be asked questions you weren't ready for. Certainly enough people had done that to me all my life.

And so, instead, I turned to him. "What now?" I asked. "Do we just...hang out in the room for the day? Until Jareth figures everything out?"

He looked at me. Then a smile crossed his face. "Not that staying in this room with you doesn't sound amazing," he said slyly and I felt my face blush hard. "But there are other...amusements in the Coven. Things we might do to pass the time."

"Like what?" I asked, suddenly curious. Then I giggled. "If you say hang gliding..."

He laughed, Then he reached out and grabbed my hand. "Come with me," he said.

And so I did.

15

"A kitchen?" I cried as we walked into the room, not able to hide the astonishment in my voice. "Why on Earth does a vampire coven have a kitchen?"

And it wasn't just any kitchen either. It was huge, with all Viking stainless steel appliances and expensive looking quartz countertops. I thought back to my barely functional kitchen at home and shook my head.

"You guys don't even eat!" I added, running my hand along the smooth countertop.

"But some of us love to cook."

I turned to Logan, surprised. He shrugged. "I was a sous chef at a Michelin starred restaurant in New York City back when I was human. Old habits die hard."

"Wow." I gave a low whistle. "I had no idea."

It was crazy, actually. I mean, not the chef thing. But the fact that he'd had this complete life before becoming a creature of the night. A normal human life—having lived more years that I had before turning. Here I kept pressing him on his sire, who had made him a vampire. As if that moment was all that mattered—and what came after it. But there was so much more to him. And that had to be part of him still.

"Well then, Chef," I said with a smile, sidling up to the breakfast bar. "What's on the menu?"

"I can whip up pretty much anything you like," he said. "But you have to assist."

Oh no. I shook my head. "Trust me, dude, you do not want my help. I, like, burn water when trying to boil it. I'd die of starvation if it weren't for delivery."

"Perhaps you have never had a good teacher," Logan said smoothly, walking over and handing me an apron. I reluctantly slipped it over my shoulders. He walked around and tied the strings. I tried and failed not to notice how his hands felt, working against the small of my back, sending a delicious shiver up my spine.

I swallowed hard, stepping forward when he had finished. Mostly to remove the urge to lean back and grind up against him. Cause that would be weird. We were cooking! There was no sex in cooking!

Also, no sex in general. Of course. Definitely none.

Though I had to admit, this guy looked pretty hot in an apron. Like disturbingly so. And here I had thought a tux was his thing. But now, looking at him moving gracefully around the kitchen, pulling out various pots and pans, I saw that he was truly in his element. He loved this kitchen. He loved making food.

My stomach growled. And I loved eating it. Time to get this show on the road.

We settled on omelets and waffles. Mostly because it felt like morning, even though it was actually nighttime. I cracked the eggs (using a trick Logan taught me to avoid getting shells in the bowl), while he chopped peppers and tomatoes.

He didn't talk much, just offered a few helpful suggestions here and there or asked me to retrieve an ingredient or two. But the silence felt comfortable rather than awkward. He was in the zone. And he was loving it. I couldn't help but keep stealing peeks at him from the corner of my eye as he worked, admiring the confidence he exuded as he deftly worked the waffle batter. As he poured it into the waffle maker and shut the top, he turned to me with a grin.

"I could have made something much fancier," he said.

"Trust me, this is perfect."

"And just think—no water was harmed in the making of this breakfast."

I laughed. "Like you said, I have a good teacher."

"The best," he agreed. Then he reached out, dragging a finger down my cheek. I gulped at the feel of his cool hand against my skin.

"Logan..." I breathed.

He pulled his finger away, holding it up for my inspection. "You had flour on your face," he said, his eyes dancing with amusement.

Oh. I felt my cheeks flush bright red. *Right.*

He stepped closer to me. Meeting my eyes with his own. He reached out again, cupping my chin in his hands, staring down at me with intense eyes.

"More...flour?" I managed to squeak out, my knees practically buckling from under me at the intensity of his gaze.

"No," he said.

Oh God. Oh God.

His hands dropped to my shoulders, massaging them gently. I bit my lower lip, so hard I probably nearly drew blood. Which, wouldn't be good in front of a vampire. Though maybe it would inspire him to kiss me.

Not that he looked as if he needed much inspiration...

"Hannah," he breathed, his full lips forming my name as if it were an actual caress. I sucked in a breath, trying to calm myself as my heart pitter-pattered like a crazy schoolgirl.

"Logan..."

BEEEP! BEEEEEEP!

We jumped apart. Logan swore under his breath. It took me a moment, in my half-dazed state to realize what was going on. What that noise was from. Then I saw the smoke.

The waffle was burning.

Logan opened the waffle maker. Sure enough, it was black. He groaned and threw it in the sink, then turned to the omelet, which wasn't in any better shape. He threw it in the sink with the waffle.

"Well," he said turning to me. "So much for your cooking lesson."

I started to laugh. I couldn't help it. For a moment Logan looked a bit offended. But then a smile spread across his face, too. And soon we were cracking up so badly we could hardly stand up. It was all so crazy, so absurd. Yet, so normal. As if I wasn't in a vampire coven, scared for my life. But on some crazy dating reality show with hilarious hijinks galore.

Finally, we settled down. Logan gazed down at the blackened dishes in the sink. "So," he said. "Shall I start again?"

"Do you have any Cheerios?" I asked. "Cause I'd be fine with that."

"*I* would not be fine with that," he shot back, giving me a scolding look. "Now sit down and let me cook for you, woman."

I obeyed, plopping down on a stool behind the breakfast bar, watching Logan start all over again. I felt bad for him, having to work to feed me. I didn't want to be high maintenance and really would have been fine with Cheerios. But I could tell he wanted to do this. And hey, who was I to turn down a home cooked meal?

It didn't take long for him to recreate the feast. He'd also added bacon this time. The extra crispy kind that I preferred. He set down the steaming plate in front of me and I breathed in the heavenly scent.

"This is amazing," I said.

His cheeks colored. "It's a simple breakfast."

"Simply amazing, you mean." I took a bite. "Oh my God," I cried. "This is so freaking good!"

He sat down next to me. For a moment he was silent. Then he said, "Do you mind if I watch you eat?" He shrugged. "I know that probably sounds weird. It's just...well, eating was one of my biggest pleasures back when I was human. And it's probably the thing I miss most."

"Ugh. I can't even imagine not being able to eat."

"Well, as I said, I can eat a little," he amended. "I mean, if I needed to keep up the appearance of being human, for example. But it all tastes like cardboard. I have no living taste buds. And I would probably throw it up later. My stomach can't digest food—only blood."

He looked so sad as he told me this. Longingly watching me put the fork to my mouth. My heart ached for him, trying to imagine what that would be like. To never taste food. Especially for someone whose life had revolved around food when he was alive. It seemed incredibly sad and incredibly unfair.

It was also something I never really considered when writing my vampire books. My vampires were so old, they barely remembered—or cared to remember—their previous lives. But for Logan, that life hadn't been so long ago. And in a way he still seemed to be grieving his humanity.

"What's wrong?" Logan asked, looking at me with concern. "You're not eating."

"Sorry," I said, taking a big forkful and shoving it into my mouth. I closed my eyes, rejoicing in the deliciousness. "I just... feel bad, making you sit there and watch me eat."

His mouth quirked. "Are you kidding? I am getting far too much pleasure watching you eat."

I blushed again. God, he had such an ability to make me blush. But I pushed on, making a playful show of my next bite. He laughed and I almost choked on the bite I was laughing so hard, too.

He reached out, taking the fork from me. The laughter died on my lips as he cut a piece of waffle, then slowly dipped it in the maple syrup. Turning to me, he reached out, presenting it to me, as he met my eyes with his own. I involuntarily licked my lips, then leaned forward, taking a bite. The sweet syrup hit my mouth, almost causing me to moan in deliciousness. Logan smiled, pulling the fork from my mouth.

"You like?" he asked.

"You have no idea," I replied. And, I suddenly realized, I wasn't just talking about the food.

I liked this. I liked all of this.

And it was fast becoming a problem how much I did.

I FINISHED EATING—WAY more food than I'd meant to and we put the dishes in the sink. I offered to wash them, but Logan assured me the Blood Coven had servants to take care of that. And why not? This place had everything else. Of course they would have help as well.

"Where to next?" I asked.

He pursed his lips together. "Do you need to write?" he queried. "I don't want you to get behind on your work on my account."

I raised my eyebrows, surprised he'd thought of that. Surprised that mattered to him. Usually no one took my deadlines seriously. I was touched that he considered this—and cared enough to ask.

"I don't have my laptop," I reminded him.

"I can get you one."

"And where would I write?"

He grinned at the question. Evidently he had something in mind. "Follow me," he said.

I did as he asked, walking with him down long underground corridors until we reached a glass door. Logan reached for the handle and pulled on it, bowing to me as it swung open.

"After you," he said.

I stepped inside the room, my jaw dropping at what was on the other side. I had assumed it would be a workspace of some sort. A vampire hotel business center, if you will. But it was so, so much more.

An indoor, underground garden. Lush and colorful with plants winding around every surface, flowers blooming brightly under artificial light. There were cobblestone paths, weaving through the greenery and little benches to sit on along the way.

"It's gorgeous!" I cried, turning back to Logan. "I had no idea!"

"It's one of my favorite places here," he admitted, stepping in behind me and closing the door. "Besides the kitchen, of course. Sometimes I come here and sit for hours, leaving the real world and all its problems far behind."

"I would totally do that," I agreed, practically skipping down the path. "How big is this place anyway?"

"It covers an entire acre."

I let out a low whistle. "That is one big secret garden."

"So you like it? Do you think you could write in here?"

"This would only be the best writing spot *ever*."

"Great. Then let me go get you a laptop so you can get started."

He turned back to the door. I watched him, feeling a slow warmth grow in my stomach. How thoughtful he was to want to let me work. To understand that I needed to write, even under these circumstances. His consideration was unlike any I'd ever gotten from a guy. And it made me want to both laugh and cry.

I swallowed hard, sinking down onto the bench. *Okay,* I scolded myself, *you really need to slow your roll. Stop getting carried away. This isn't some romance novel. This is real life. And it's becoming a real problem.*

The thought sobered me and I clasped my hands on my lap, trying to get my emotions back in check. Yes, this had been a delicious fantasy. But the reason we were here was because we were in danger. There were people out there—no, not people—vampires out there—who wanted to kill us.

But, I realized, that wasn't really the biggest problem. The far bigger problem was how my feelings were growing for Logan. I had just met the guy, for God's sake. And suddenly I was feeling all warm and gooey every time he opened his mouth. Yes, he was handsome. Yes, he was exciting. Yes, he was sweet and tender and kind. And considerate. But he was practically a stranger. Also, an immortal vampire. A vampire capable of vampire scent —which could draw a person under his thrall. For all I knew that was all this was. Me, seduced by a supernatural predator. Lulled into a false sense of safety and security. I barely knew this guy but I had put my entire life in his hands. I had allowed myself to feel for him more than I'd felt for anyone in years.

It was dangerous. It was stupid. It was what I'd sworn off for good. And I needed to keep that promise for myself. Or I was sure to get hurt. And I didn't know if I could take any more hurt.

Logan returned a moment later, carrying a very nice laptop. I took it from him, muttering a thank you, but refusing to meet his eyes. I could feel his frown as he looked down at me.

"What's wrong?" he asked in a worried tone.

"Nothing," I shot back. I pursed my lips together. "Um, I actually prefer to write alone."

"Oh. Right. Of course." He raked a hand through his hair. "I'll, um, let you get to it then."

I could hear the hurt in his voice, mixed with confusion. He could clearly feel the change in the air, in my demeanor and it killed me to disappoint him. But at the same time, it was better for both of us. Better to rip off the Band-Aid now than let this—thing—whatever it was, fester between us.

"I'm going to take a walk," he said, his voice stiff. "I hope you get a lot of writing done."

And with that, he left me, going deeper into the garden. I watched him go, then turned back to my laptop, pulling it open. I clicked on Microsoft Word and started to type.

But the words wouldn't come. I couldn't lose myself in my fantasy world. Not with my real one pounding at the edges of my brain. Not with Logan wandering just out of sight in this beautiful underground garden.

For years all I cared about were my stories. They'd been more important to me than my actual life. But now, there was something else. Something more captivating than words on a page.

Make that some*one*.

I didn't take risks. That was what I always told Darla. It was my mantra. Wrapped in stubborn pride. As if that made me an interesting person—my lack of being interesting. Really, it had been nothing more than a shield. To protect me from any possible hurt. Yet at the same time, my shield had also been my prison. And in addition to not getting hurt, I didn't get better, either. That night Jake had violated my body. Now, years later, he was still violating my mind. Taking away my freedom, my chance at happiness. Forcing me to push away people who cared about me.

Logan had done nothing but treat me with respect and care. And I had treated him like he was just another Jake. I tried to tell myself it was because he was a vampire, but I knew deep down that wasn't truly it. It was because he was a man. And I had allowed Jake to lock me up in a tower, a willing damsel in distress.

Which wasn't fair. It was so not fair.

I set down the laptop. I rose to my feet. Took a step, then another. Slowly at first, then quickening. Until I was running down the path, my eyes darting down every turn or fork. My heart was in my throat. Tears were streaming down my face. But I kept running.

I found him standing in front of the most beautiful fountain. Made of stone with elegant carvings of fairies and flowers. Crisp, clean water cascaded from a bucket above, into the small pool, making a loud splashing sound.

I stood there for a moment, watching him watch the water. Taking in his broad shoulders, his trim waist, his powerful torso and muscular legs. But that wasn't what sent the shiver of desire driving through me. Yes, he was a perfect physical specimen. But he was so much more than that, too.

I opened my mouth, then closed it again. Feeling suddenly stupid and hot and dumb. What was I going to say? How was I going to explain? Was he going to get annoyed with me? This hot and cold thing I had going on with him? How could I convince him that this time I really meant it. Especially when I wasn't a hundred percent sure I did?

I turned and started to walk away. This had been an ill thought out idea, I told myself. I needed to reassess before I did something I would regret. Get a handle on my emotions. Come back to my senses again.

But as I took a step I accidentally kicked a rock, which rolled into another with a loud knocking sound. I froze. Then sheepishly turned around. Logan was staring at me.

"Did you...need something?" he asked in a tight voice.

I swallowed hard, my mind racing with a million things to say. The fear pricking at me, telling me I had one last chance to wimp out. To walk away.

But I shook my head. No. Not this time.

"Yes," I said simply. "I need something."

"And what, may I ask, do you need?"

I met his eyes. "You."

16

*H*e stared at me for a moment. A long, agonizing moment. I tried to read the expression on his face, but I couldn't. Was he annoyed? Angry? Frustrated?

"I'm sorry," I blurted out. "That was dumb. I shouldn't of--"

He was on me in a heartbeat. So fast I couldn't see him move. One moment he was by the fountain and the next I was in his arms. His mouth on mine with a hard, bruising kiss. His hands wrapped in my hair. I moaned as the pleasure shot through me. As he shoved me against the garden wall, he pressed his body against mine, as if he couldn't get close enough. As if he wanted to crawl inside of me and make our two bodies one. Desire radiated off his skin, making his normally cold flesh scorching to my touch.

I wrapped my arms around his chest, his unabashed passion making me feel brave. Then I dropped my hands down to cup his backside. He groaned in appreciation, his knee slipping between my thighs. His hands dropping to my shoulders, his thumbs skimming the tips of my breasts. I shuddered as a shock of pleasure rippled through me like wildfire and I gasped against his mouth.

In an instant, he pulled away. Looked down at me, his beautiful eyes filled with questions. "Is this...okay?" he murmured huskily. "I can stop. I mean, if you're not ready..."

I bit my lower lip. "No," I said. "Don't stop. I'm ready."

His mouth curved into the most beautiful smile. His eyes radiated his lust and desire. He leaned down, scooping me up into his arms as if I weighed nothing at all. Then he carried me over to a bed of flowers and laid me down. The heady scent of roses mixed with his own woodsy scent made my head spin. But in a good way this time. The best way.

"Oh Logan," I said, reaching up to stroke his cheek. He smiled against my hand, then took it in his own and kissed my palm.

"Hannah," he said. And it was all that he needed to say.

I woke up sometime later, still swaddled in the flowerbed, our legs and bodies entwined with one another. The poor flowers were the real victims here, crushed from our enthusiastic coming together. But it had been worth their sacrifice. For the first time in as long as I could remember, I felt no fear.

And I didn't want to cut.

"You're awake," Logan observed with a smile, reaching out to stroke my hair. I nodded.

"Were you sleeping?" I asked.

"I rarely sleep during the night," he explained. "Only day."

"Oh." I blushed, realizing that I had passed out, essentially trapping him there while I slept. "Sorry. I didn't mean to--"

He put a finger to my lips. "Trust me," he said in a husky voice. "I liked lying here, watching you sleep." He paused, than added, "Yeah, that came out creepier than I meant it to."

"Okay Edward Cullen," I teased. He laughed, sitting up and

running his hand through his already tousled hair. He was still shirtless and it was all I could do not to run my hand down his magnificent chest. Start things up all over again.

But my stomach had other ideas.

"What time is it?" I asked, grabbing my shirt and pulling it over my head.

He glanced at his watch. "Almost morning."

"Wow. I slept half the night?"

"You've had a rough couple of days. I'm glad you were able to get some sleep."

"Yeah. Me too." I pursed my lips, then dared look up at him. "You know, if I had known running for my life from vampire slayers was so fun, I'd have done it a long time ago."

His expression sobered. "What?" I asked, a bit fearfully.

He rose to his feet. Grabbed his pants and shucked them on. "I should go talk to Jareth," he said. "Find out if he learned anything about our situation tonight."

I nodded. The concerned look on his face made the warmness of our earlier coupling cool a little. We'd been hiding out here, away from real life. But we couldn't do that forever. The Blood Coven was only a temporary refuge. Eventually we'd have to leave. And when we did...

"I'll come with you," I said, hastily getting dressed.

But Logan shook his head. "No," he said. Then he added, "I'm sorry. It's just...we have our ways. And humans are not allowed to know them."

"Oh." I felt a sinking disappointment inside of me. I knew it was ridiculous—just because I'd hooked up with Logan didn't mean I was suddenly a vampire and part of the gang. I was a girlfriend at best, but far from an equal partner.

Logan gave me a sorry look. "Come on," he said. "Let me take you to our media room while you wait. We have every movie under the sun. You can veg out and eat popcorn while I figure things out."

"Sure," I said. Because what else could I say?

Logan peered at me. "You're upset," he observed.

"No." I shook my head. "I'm just a little worried. I appreciate you trying to fix everything. I just wish I could be more help."

He pulled me into his arms. I collapsed against his chest, trying not to sob. I didn't want to be that girl, that helpless girl who needed a guy to save her. But then I also didn't want to be that stubborn girl who went against all common sense and made things worse.

"You have no idea how much help you are," Logan whispered in my ear. And he sounded so sincere, I felt a little better.

He took me to the media room, which was actually more like a small movie theater. He set me up with a big bowl of buttery popcorn and large soda and handed me the remote. Then he leaned down, kissing the top of my head.

"I had an amazing night," he whispered.

I smiled up at him. "Me too," I said. "We should do this more often." I paused, then added, "I mean, the fun part. Not the hiding out for our lives part."

"Let me see what I can do about that," he said. "I'll be back."

I WAS asleep when Logan returned. I felt his hand on me, gently shaking me awake. I opened my eyes, blinking at him sleepily. Then a smile crossed my face. "Hey," I said. "You're back."

He nodded slowly. There was something in his eyes. Something that resembled pain. I sat up, frowning.

"What's wrong?"

He shook his head. "Nothing," he said. "It's just...almost

morning. I need to get back to the room to sleep. I didn't know if I should just leave you here or..."

"I'll come back with you," I said, standing up.

He nodded and together we walked back to our shared bedroom. Logan was quiet on the way, which worried me a little.

"What happened?" I asked. "Did you talk to Jareth?"

He nodded. "You don't have to worry anymore," he said. "I've straightened everything out."

"You did?" I cried. "That's awesome."

He gave me a small smile. But I noticed it didn't quite meet his eyes. "Yes," he said. "Awesome."

We reached the room. As he closed the door behind us, I opened my mouth to ask more questions. Get more details. But Logan didn't seem in the mood to talk. Instead, he stepped toward me, a haunted look in his eyes. Before I could ask what was wrong, he took my face in his hands, drawing me to him. Kissing me with a desperation that took my breath away.

Still kissing me, walked me over to the bed, laying me down. Then he climbed on top of me, dragging a hand down my side. I reached up, digging my fingers into his thick hair.

"Oh Hannah," he groaned against my mouth.

Suffice to say, no one slept in the chair that morning.

17

*W*hen I woke up, I noticed three things in quick succession.

One: I was in my own bed.

Two: It was daytime, the sun streaming through my window.

Three: Logan was nowhere to be seen.

Unexpected panic slammed through me with a force of a ten-ton truck. I jerked up in bed, looking around. Everything was there, everything familiar. Yet for some reason it also looked foreign. As if it belonged to a previous life. A previous me.

I swung my feet around, out of bed. My eyes still searching for something—anything—to prove the night before wasn't just some dream. Then my eyes locked onto a stack of papers by my computer. A printout. I ran over to it, grabbing it with trembling hands.

It was my manuscript. The pages I'd written while at Logan's safe house. I nearly collapsed into my chair in relief. It wasn't a dream.

Though...shouldn't I have wanted it to have been one? We were running for our lives. Slayer, Inc. hot on our heels. My life was in danger. Was my life *still* in danger?

Dropping the manuscript, I searched the surface of my desk. Finally, I found what I was looking for—praying for.

A note from Logan.

Dear Hannah,

I hope you had a restful sleep. Please once again accept my apologies for stealing you away and I hope I didn't put you too far behind in your work. In any case, I have been successful in making a deal. The vampires understand that you are innocent. They will not come after you.

I will never forget our time together. Thank you for being such a light in my dark life.

Yours,

Logan

PS Your vampires are fantastic. Don't change a fucking thing. I only hope that my real life kind can live up to your beautiful imagination.

I STARED AT THE NOTE, my heart pounding in my chest. My stomach swimming with a mixture of longing and fear. I turned it over, hoping there was more, but knowing there wouldn't be. There wouldn't be anything more.

I would never see him again.

It didn't say that in the note. But it seemed implied. This was a final farewell. A Dear John letter, vampire style. It was easy to read between the lines. I was to go back to my old life. And forget any of the underworld I'd seen existed.

I dropped the letter, tears streaming down my cheeks. I angrily brushed them away. What was wrong with me? I should be thrilled, ecstatic. I had been given a second chance. I no longer had to fear for my life from some rogue Buffy the Vampire Slayer.

So why was I so damned sad instead?

I stared down at the letter, reading it again. Trying to picture Logan writing it while I slept. Did he glance over at me once or twice as he wrote? Did anything stir in his heart as he did?

Stupid. I crumbled up the note, tossing it in the trash. *Pathetic. What did you expect? A vampire to fall in love with you overnight? He was practically a prince. And you—you are nothing but a pathetic rape victim recluse with self-mutilation issues. What would he possibly want with someone like you?*

I found myself diving in the trash to retrieve the letter, smoothing it out on my lap as the tears fell onto the paper, blurring the ink. I set it aside, out of the splash zone, then glanced over at my box. My Carpathian puzzle box. But then I shook my head. I wasn't going to do that. Hopefully ever again. If anything positive could come from the last nights, it could at least be that.

My cell phone startled me out of my reverie. Loud, piercing —when had I turned up the volume? Usually I kept it on vibrate. I dove for it, heart in my throat, praying it was someone that I knew it wouldn't be.

Someone I would never hear from again.

Instead it was Darla. A very relieved Darla who had evidently been calling me fifty-thousand times since the party. She told me she'd left her concert early to come find me there, feeling guilty she'd allowed me to attend alone. When no one knew where I was, she'd panicked. She'd come to my house; she'd banged on my door. At one point she'd even called the police to report me missing.

She was talking so fast I barely was able to get a word in.

When I did, I simply apologized. Blamed my depression. Told her the party had been too much for me and I had fled it and hid in bed for the last thirty-six hours, having turned off my phone. Sadly, this excuse was so believable, coming from my mouth, that she believed it without much question. Though she did repeat her desire for me to seek help. But then, there was nothing odd about that.

I finally got her off the phone, promising I would answer the door when the car service came to pick me up tonight. In all the craziness, I had forgotten that I was technically still on tour. Still expected to be at a neighboring bookstore to celebrate the Jonathan and Maisie chronicles with adoring fans.

I glanced over to my bookshelf. At all the copies of those books.

I only hope that my real life kind can live up to your beautiful imagination.

Logan's words echoed through my head, as if he'd whispered them in my ear instead of putting them to paper. I closed my eyes, remembering the feel of his cool hands all over my flushed skin. His hard mouth pressing against my own. What was it he said again in that bookstore? *Real men don't kiss with the gentleness of a butterfly's wing.*

A smile crept over my face. He hadn't been wrong about that.

But now...now it was over. Cinderella was back from the ball. Back in the rags of her own pathetic existence, created by her own hand. I looked around my apartment, remembering how much I used to love it here. How safe and secure I felt.

Now it resembled a prison.

I rose to my feet. Walked mechanically to the kitchen to make myself some coffee. I grabbed a granola bar and ripped it open. Chewed it while waiting for the coffee to brew. Then I grabbed my BB8 shaped mug and poured my coffee into it before heading over to my computer.

It was what I did every morning. A ritual I quite enjoyed. But today it brought me no happiness. And as I stared at the blank screen, I was given no words. Jonathan was not whispering in my ear anymore.

It was all Logan. But he had nothing left to say.

18

The bookstore was packed. Not surprising I supposed. They always were. The crowds pressed against one another, clutching copies of my new release in their hands. As I took my seat, they broke out into applause, as if I had performed a trick, rather than made them wait an extra fifteen minutes while I desperately gathered my nerves in the store's back office.

I forced a smile to my lips as I scanned the room. Many of the readers had come in costume tonight—probably due to the close proximity to Halloween. There were dozens of Maisies in her signature flowing red gown. And almost as many Jonathans, in their dashing Victorian formalwear.

I felt a slow ache grow, deep inside as I remembered how magical it used to feel—to see the crowds dressed up like this. To know my simple words had inspired such devotion—such sincere fandom.

But now it just seemed like a joke somehow. Kids playing at dress-up, with no idea what they were really doing. What was really out there and how they acted in real life. As Logan had said, real vampires did not dress as holdouts from Victorian England. They lived amongst us, dressed like us. Of course they would want to fit in. The last thing they needed was some ridiculous costume to draw attention to their pale skin. Their catlike movement. Their "otherness."

"Are you ready?" Darla asked, peering at me with concern. I blushed realizing I must have appeared in a trance. I'd been practically a zombie all day and I knew I was beginning to worry her. And so I nodded at her, then cleared my throat. Leaning into the microphone to begin my talk. Trying to make this as normal as possible. Not to mention quick. The sooner I got back to my apartment the better.

I gave a brief introduction, then I read from my book. Then Darla opened it up to questions and I answered best I could without giving away any spoilers. But my heart was not in any of it. In fact, it was almost as if someone else was in my body, going through the motions and I was having some out-of-body experience watching from above. It all seemed so stupid, so mundane. So pointless.

Logan was out there somewhere. A real vampire. And I was wasting my life celebrating a cardboard cutout with fangs.

Was he okay? I wondered for about the billionth time today as I finished the Q&A and Darla invited readers to come forward to get their books signed. He had mentioned a deal he'd made. One to keep me safe. But he had said nothing of his own safety. What if he'd turned himself in? What if he was going to face trial? What if he was convicted of killing that other vampire and was sentenced to eternal death for doing it?

I would never know. I could live my entire life not knowing what happened to him.

Except...I couldn't. Wouldn't. I needed to know. To know he was safe. That he had made his case and was no longer accused. That he was out there, somewhere, cooking and singing karaoke and living his best vampire life. Even if we couldn't be together, I needed to know he was okay. After all, it was my fault he was in this mess to begin with.

I felt the girl standing before me shift uncomfortably. I looked up. "Um," I stammered. "What's your name again?" She was dressed like Maisie. But her costume was cheap. Home-made. She had gotten the buttons wrong. I shook my head. So what? It was just a silly costume.

"Mandy," she said, looking a little annoyed. I blushed as I realized her name was already in the book, a little sticky note in Darla's handwriting. This was how we did it, so I would know how to spell the names properly.

"Right. Of course. Sorry." I scribbled something in her book. Then I handed it back to her.

"Are you okay?" she asked, peering at me with concern.

"Um, yeah. Sorry. Just a little tired."

"She's fine," Darla butted in. "Now if you want a picture, make it quick. We've got a lot of people to get through."

The girl—Mandy—did want a picture and so I posed, baring my teeth in my best recreation of a smile. Then Mandy said goodbye, that it was a true honor to meet me. And I felt a little guilty that I had basically slept walked through our entire encounter. A meeting she claimed she would remember for the rest of her life. And it had barely registered in my troubled brain.

She walked away and the next reader stepped up to the desk. I signed his book. I took a photo. He walked away. Over and over, rinse and repeat. The seemingly never-ending line snaking through the bookstore. I signed and signed, trying to keep focused. To not think about how pathetically unimportant this all was. Mundane and useless. Here I was, signing books about vampires. When a real vampire might be in danger—because of me.

I had made it about halfway through the line when the

sensation came over me. A sudden feeling that something was wrong. I looked up, just in time to catch a strange movement by the door. Almost a blur, hard to see. The hairs of my neck stood on end and a chill tripped down my spine. My heart pounded in my chest and I tried to tell myself I was jumping at shadows.

But then I saw it again. Closer this time. Was there someone there? Someone from the other world?

And, if so, what did they want?

Panic seized me. What if it was Slayer, Inc.? What if Logan's deal fell through and now I was back on their hit list. I was vulnerable here. A sitting duck. They could swoop in and take me away.

I dropped my pen. It fell to the floor with a clatter. Pushing back on my chair, I rose to my feet.

"Hannah! What are you doing?"

I could hear Darla's voice. But it sounded as if it was coming from a vacuum. Far away and muffled. I shook my head.

"I...I have to go."

"Now? But we have at least another hour left. All these people have been waiting—"

"I'm sorry. They'll have to come back. I have to go! Now!"

And with that, I turned and fled the bookstore. I could hear the dismayed fans behind me. Their protests. They'd been waiting in line for hours, some of them. And I felt truly bad for disappointing them.

But I couldn't help it. I had to get out of there. Now.

Though where I would go, I had no idea.

19

I ended up having the driver take me home. I had nowhere else to go. Darla kept calling my phone until finally I turned it off. I knew I shouldn't worry her like that. But what was my alternative? Tell her I was afraid I was being stalked by a vampire slayer? Yeah, that would have gone over well.

Back at home, I locked all the windows and doors. Set the alarm. But that didn't stop my heart from racing. My gaze darting to every corner of the apartment. If Slayer, Inc. could infiltrate a vampire compound, surely they'd have no problem breaking into my little apartment.

I paced the living room, not sure what to do. Several times I considered going to my Carpathian puzzle box, in an attempt to calm my nerves. But I was determined not to do that anymore. And also, what if it wasn't Slayer, Inc. who was after me? What if it were another vampire coven? They'd pick up the scent of my blood. Which was the last thing I needed now.

I read Logan's note over again, for the millionth time, wishing he'd left his phone number. Some way to contact him, to let him know what I feared was going on. Maybe he would have come. Maybe he would have at least sent someone else to come. As it was, I had no one to turn to. I was alone.

I pulled my shades closed. As if that would help. Then I started to pick up the apartment. Useless, I know, but the only distraction I could think of. I couldn't cut. And there was no way I could write. No way to lose myself in a fantasy, when a dark reality was lurking close by, waiting to strike.

I grabbed my clothes off the floor. The ones I'd worn the night before. As I walked them over to my washing machine, something fell out of one of the pockets. A slip of paper. I picked it up, frowning, at first not recognizing what it was. Then my eyes widened as I read the front of the card, the memory reigniting in my brain.

Rayne MacDonald, the card read.

My number one fan.

Call me if you need anything, she'd insisted. *Anything at all.*

Hands trembling, I dove for my purse. Pulled out my phone. Turned it back on. It rang immediately. Darla, of course. This time I answered.

"I'm fine!" I barked into the phone, not bothering with hellos. "You don't have to worry!"

"Don't have to worry? Hannah, you ran from the book signing like the devil himself was at your heels."

I winced. She wasn't wrong.

"I had a panic attack," I explained lamely. Thankfully it wasn't a far stretch for me and thus believable. "The walls were closing in. But I'm okay now. I'm home. I'm safe." I drew in a breath. "Please tell the bookstore I am so sorry. That I will reschedule—any night they want me back, I'll be there."

Darla was silent for a moment. Then, "Are you sure you're okay? You sound out of breath."

"I'm fine. Really. I just...ran to the phone. I'd been charging it. It had run out of charge. That's why I didn't answer before."

The lies flew from my lips before I could even acknowledge them. Ridiculous, too convenient to be true. I knew Darla probably only half believed me anyway. But she would support me all the same. She always did, I thought guiltily. Even when I didn't deserve her to.

"Okay," she said at last. "But I'm coming over. Once I wrap up at the store. Leave the door open in case you fall asleep."

Shit. "Okay," I said, not able to come up with any excuse why she shouldn't. "Take your time though. I'm totally fine."

"I'll be the judge of that."

I frowned a little. Was I that much of a child? That she felt she always had to take care of me? That I couldn't deal with life on my own? Make my own decisions? Find my own way? If only she knew what I'd gone through the nights before. She might realize I could handle myself pretty well in a crisis after all.

I shook my head. Time to think of such things later. Right now I had a phone call to make.

I said goodbye to Darla, then dialed Rayne's number. It rang three times and I was starting to worry she wouldn't pick up. Then...

"Hello?" I could hear loud music in the background practically drowning out the voice.

I let out a breath of relief. "Rayne?" I asked. "This is Hannah."

"Hannah...?" I could hear the doubt in her voice.

"Hannah Miller," I added. "You know, the writer?"

"Oh my God!" she cried. "Hannah Miller! Of course! I'm so sorry! I just—well, I never thought you'd call!" Even over the loud music I could hear the excitement in her voice. "But I'm so glad you did! I have been freaking out since I met you. I can't believe you were at the Blood Coven. How'd the research go anyway?"

"Um, about that."

"Yeah?"

I bit my lower lip. "Can we meet somewhere? To talk?"

"Of course! I always have time for my favorite writer. When do you want to meet?"

"Is now too soon?"

"Nope. I'm at Club Fang. Can you get here?"

"I think so."

"Awesome. Just text me when you get there. I'll make sure we have a quiet room to talk in."

I agreed and hung up the phone, my heart pattering in my chest all over again. Club Fang. Had I really just committed to going to Club Fang tonight? Back to the scene of the crime? I wondered if I should call her back. Tell her I wanted to meet somewhere else.

But something inside me prevented me from redialing her number. Something small and niggling at the back of my brain.

Maybe Logan would be there.

My heart skipped a beat at the thought.

And I knew I was going to go.

But what to wear? I had stuck out like a sore thumb last time I went to Club Fang and I didn't want to do that again. I needed something cool. Something that would help me blend in with the gothy crowd. So I wouldn't call attention to myself if Slayer, Inc. was lurking nearby.

But when I looked in my closet I saw nothing that would work. It was all yoga pants, cotton t-shirts. God, was I really this boring in real life?

But just as I was about to give up and resign myself to jeans and a black t-shirt, I saw the dress. At the very back of my closet, almost hidden from view.

It was crimson. A beautiful ball gown. With a full skirt, plunging neckline and no sleeves. Pretty much straight off the cover of *Blood and Roses,* the book that had started it all. The dress had been given to me as a gift from Darla the time I was signed up to go to DragonCon. She had told me that everyone there cosplayed. That I could play Maisie and it would be so much fun.

In the end, I had chickened out. I was too stressed out to go so far out of my comfort zone. To wear a costume so dramatic. Besides, who wanted to see my bare arms? The ugly silver scars and fresh scabs marring my skin. And so I had stuffed the dress in the back of my closet. And I had never looked at it again.

But now...

"Okay, Miller," I muttered under my breath. "Let's do this."

Time to channel my inner Maisie. And find out what the hell was going on.

---

20

*B*y the time I arrived, Club Fang was going off, with the place as packed as it had been the night I showed up with Logan—maybe even more so. As I let the valet take my car away, I wondered belatedly, if I'd even be able to get in, what with the line winding around the block. On Logan's arm I was able to walk right up to the front of the line. But me, by myself...

No. I squared my shoulders. Lifted my chin. I could do this. I was dressed to kill and channeling my inner Maisie. And Maisie would never let some silly velvet rope stand in her way of getting to Logan.

I meant, Rayne. Getting to Rayne. Which was why I was here.

Argh.

Drawing in a breath, I sauntered up to the bouncer. Trying to look cool, calm and collected even as I was this close to eating it on the pavement with these high heels. I could feel the stares of the other patrons in line on me as I walked past them, but I kept my eyes on the prize. When I arrived at the front door, the bouncer was in the process of letting a girl with a rather elaborate nose ring inside. When he saw me, his hand froze on the rope. His mouth practically dropped open. I hid a small grin. *Thank you, Darla.* The dress was doing its job.

"Hey! I thought it was our turn!" the girl in line protested as the bouncer clicked the rope closed again. She set her blood red lips in a pout, giving me a look of death. But the bouncer ignored her, his eyes locked on me.

"I'm here for Rayne McDonald," I said, trying to keep my voice from quavering with nervousness. "She's expecting me."

The bouncer nodded. He opened the rope for me. I gave him a sweet smile and sauntered through. As I passed the look-of-death girl, I gave her the finger. So un-Hannah like it wasn't even funny. And yet so satisfying at the same time. Maybe I should channel Maisie more often.

The club, it turned out, was as packed inside as it was outside. Lights were flashing. Dancers were gyrating to dark, techno beats. I pushed past them, holding up my skirts to avoid being stepped on. I could feel people's fascinated stares as I crossed the room. Maybe this outfit was a bit too much.

Okay, definitely too much. But kind of amazing at the same time.

"There you are! I almost didn't recognize you!"

A voice behind me made me turn. My eyes fell on Rayne who was nodding her head appreciatively. "You look fucking amazing," she said with a low whistle. "Seriously, when this is all over, you *must* let me borrow that dress."

I snorted. "You can have it," I told her. "It's really not my thing."

"I can assure you, luv. That is *definitely* your thing."

I whirled around to see a tall, blond vampire step in behind me. He looked like a young Jude Law. Super cute. Rayne rolled her eyes and smacked him in his stomach.

"Down Jareth," she scolded. "You're mine, remember?"

The vampire grinned naughtily, then leaned over to kiss

Rayne on the top of her head. "So you keep reminding me," he teased. But the way he looked at her told me she had nothing to worry about. He was completely smitten. Must be nice. To have someone to look at you like that.

Which brought me to my reason for being here.

"Can we talk somewhere private?" I asked.

"Yes! I reserved a room in the back. Come on." Rayne grabbed my hand and dragged me to the back of the club. Jareth trailed behind us. And suddenly I realized why his name seemed so familiar. Jareth had been the name of the Blood Coven Master that Logan went to see. Was this the same Jareth? Was he really some vampire king?

And, if so, could he help me now?

We headed to the back of the club, through the VIP entrance and into the feeding rooms. Rayne grabbed a key off the wall and walked over to room number seven, unlocking it and pulling it open.

"After you," she said with a mock bow.

I stepped inside, suddenly feeling a little weirded out. And who could blame me? I was literally going into a bloodletting room in a vampire club with two vampires. One who may or may not be an obsessed fan. What if she had this idea that she wanted to drink my blood? Maybe she thought it would give her some insight into the plot of the next book?

I shook my head. While that was a pretty cool plot idea for a future novel, it seemed pretty unlikely in real life.

I looked around the room. It was sparse, but clean. I didn't know what I had expected. Maybe some blood stains on the wall? But it might as well have been a hospital room. Well-lit, with a small table and two comfy looking armchairs. Rayne and Jareth squeezed into one chair, getting cozy together, while I took the other, my dress fanning out as I plopped down.

"That dress though!" Rayne said, giving a low whistle. "Where did you even find such a magnificent thing?"

"Now Rayne. I don't think she came all this way to discuss fashion," Jareth admonished gently.

Rayne rolled her eyes. "Okay fun police," she groaned. Then she turned back to me. "So," she said. "What seems to be the problem?"

I drew in a breath. Here went nothing.

"Last night," I said, "I feel asleep at Hotel Blood Coven or whatever. But when I woke up, I was back in my old bed. Logan was gone and all that was left was this note he'd written, saying he was going to take care of everything. And that I wouldn't be in any danger from Slayer, Inc."

"I like how he takes all the credit for that," Rayne muttered before Jareth hushed her.

I bit my lower lip. "Anyway, I was at my book signing tonight when I suddenly felt this...*something*. Something odd that I couldn't quite put my finger one. Like there was someone in the room I couldn't see. A sound I couldn't quite hear. It was the weirdest feeling. I don't think anyone else felt it." I frowned, my heart pounding all over again as I remembered the scene. "I got out of there as fast as I could and headed home. But I still didn't feel safe. And since I didn't have Logan's contact info, I tried you." I shrugged. "That's pretty much it."

I caught Rayne and Jareth exchanging looks. "What?" I demanded. "Do you know something I don't? Do you think Slayer, Inc. could be after me, after all?"

"Very unlikely," Rayne replied. "I went to their headquarters yesterday to ask them to lay off. But they told me you weren't a target. And I doubt anything has changed since then."

Oh. I frowned, my head spinning in confusion at this news. I should have been relieved. But for some reason I felt even more disconcerted. I mean, was I wrong about all of this? Had it only been my own anxiety acting up back at the bookstore? My over-reaching imagination conjuring up a book-worthy third act to my date with a vampire?

But no. I shook my head. I had felt it. It had been there—whatever it was. It was real.

I turned back to the vampires, realizing Jareth was speaking.

"Honestly," he said. "What you are describing does not sound like Slayer, Inc. Most Slayer, Inc. operatives are human. You would see them coming a mile away."

I looked at Rayne. "You're not human," I pointed out.

"I also would never stake you," she shot back, not missing a beat. "You've got too many books to write before you head off to the great pizza place in the sky."

"Right." I made a face. "So, not Slayer, Inc.," I said. "Then...who?"

Jareth leaned forward in his chair, his eyes locked on me. "Sounds to me like you're being hunted by a vampire."

21

A vampire.

I leaned back in my chair, my stomach swimming with unease. I mean, it wasn't as if I hadn't already considered this as a possibility—even back at the bookstore. But to hear it said out loud. But another vampire.

"Oh God," I murmured.

Jareth gave me a pitying look. "I'm sorry," he said. "You should not be involved in any of this. Logan should have never brought you here to begin with. It was a foolish vanity."

I frowned, everything inside of me suddenly wanting to stand up for Logan. To tell Jareth he wasn't to blame. But what good would that do? I had to focus on the more impending threat. Once that was taken care of, we could Monday morning quarterback all the rest.

I leaned forward in my chair. "Who's after me?" I demanded.

"I'm not sure," Jareth replied. "But I think it could be a group of...well, let's just call them vigilantes."

"*Vampire* vigilantes," Rayne added helpfully. "Which, by the way, could totally be a thing in your next book, don't you think?"

Jareth shot her a warning look before turning back to me.

"Look," he said. "I don't know how much Logan told you, but the vampire he killed outside of Club Fang was a key witness in the parole hearing for the vampire Pyrus, the former leader of our Consortium."

"And do we want him out or no?" I asked.

"No way," Rayne replied. "He needs to rot in there forever. Especially seeing all the trouble it was for me to put him away in the first place." She made a face. "God, he was the worst."

"Unfortunately, not everyone agrees with Rayne," Jareth continued. "And even in prison, Pyrus still retains quite a large base. A group of vampires who have left their old covens to form a new group that preaches the old ways, just as Pyrus once did. They're not content to live in the shadows of humanity. They want to take over. To rule the world and make humans their blood slaves."

"Now *that* sounds like a book plot," I muttered.

"Unfortunately, it's all too real," Jareth replied. "And they have to be furious about Logan killing the one guy who could help spring their fearless leader from prison."

I winced, my insides squirming. Here I had been so worried about being tracked down by rogue vampires myself, I hadn't really considered that Logan would be their true target. He'd talked about making a deal—I'd thought it was with Slayer, Inc. The police department—basically. Not a group of vampire baddies out for blood. I had thought he would stand trial. In a courtroom. With a lawyer. But this...

What had he promised them in exchange for my freedom? Would he have sacrificed himself—made a deal with the devils —to keep me safe?

I felt sick to my stomach. I looked up at Rayne and Jareth.

"Is Logan okay?" I blurted out. "I mean, they didn't actually get him, right?"

"You don't think he would have..." Rayne started, then dropped off, giving Jareth a meaningful look.

Jareth shook his head. "No. He wouldn't do that. That would be a huge violation."

"Violation?" I interrupted. "What violation?" My heart was pounding now. I didn't know what they were talking about, but the looks on their faces told me it was not good.

Rayne turned to me, a worried look on her face. "Sorry," she said. "Vampire politics are super complicated. But basically if a coven has a problem with someone from another coven, they apply to work through it publically. Through consortium meetings, maybe a trial." She paused, then added, "They are not to take matters into their own hands. Ever."

I swallowed hard. "But you think Logan did."

"I specifically ordered him not to," Jareth said. "It would have been a terrible move, even with a law-abiding coven. But this faction, well, they aren't exactly known for rule-following."

I nodded stiffly, even as fear spun down my spine. I didn't know what to say. I thought back to the letter. Logan saying he'd take care of things...

"I bet he turned himself in," Rayne piped up. "Maybe made a bargain? You know, to keep them away from Hannah?"

"If he did, then he is stupider than I thought," Jareth growled. He pulled out his cell phone and sent a text message. I watched, waiting breathlessly, my heart in my throat. I so wanted him to look up and tell me everything was okay. That Logan was actually back at home, cooking in his kitchen, just for the fun of it. Or in the Blood Coven, strolling through the gardens.

But then Jareth's face darkened. He jerked to his feet.

"What?" I demanded, horror coursing through me. Though, of course, I could make a pretty good guess what he was going to say.

"That fool." Jareth swore under his breath. "That goddamned fool." He turned to Rayne. "Take Hannah back to the Blood Coven. I need to call an emergency meeting with Lord Magnus and the Consortium leaders. This could be a big problem."

"What? No! I want to come with you!" Rayne protested.

He shook his head. "I need you to keep Hannah safe," he said. "If anything happens to her—a mortal—it could raise the attention of Slayer, Inc. for real this time. And I do not need to deal with them, on top of everything else."

Rayne sighed. "Fine," she said. She flashed me an apologetic look. "Guess it's back to the Blood Coven for us." She rose to her feet, giving Jareth a quick kiss on the cheek. "Go save the world, baby," she teased. "We ladies will just sit back and clutch our pearls."

Jareth sighed loudly, but kissed the top of her head. Then he headed out of the room, closing the door behind him. Rayne watched him go for a moment, then turned to me, a mischievous grin on her face. I cocked my head in question.

"What?" I started to ask. Then I stopped. "We're not going to the Blood Coven, are we?" I realized aloud.

"Yeah, not so much," she said.

"So...then...?"

She slapped me on the back. "Come on," she said. "Let's go save your boyfriend."

We left Club Fang. I drove since Rayne had come with Jareth and had no car of her own. Which wouldn't have been a big deal except that her directions were terrible and she kept flipping through my satellite radio, searching for a particular station that I wasn't sure, by the end of the trip, even existed. She talked a lot, too. Mostly about her feelings for the characters and storylines in my book. That said, she didn't expect much of a response from my end. Which was good, seeing as I was so distraught I could barely drive, never mind argue plot points with an obsessive fan.

All I could think of was Logan. Where he was. What he had bargained. If he was okay. If he was still even alive. Well, vampire alive anyway. Would I ever see him again? Would he ever hold me in his arms, stroking my hair? Whispering in my ear. Telling me everything would be okay.

It was funny; I had been alone for so long. And I had never minded the solitude. But now, thinking of a lifetime without Logan seemed interminable torture.

We had to find him. We just had to.

Finally, after what seemed an eternity, we pulled up outside a dark, spooky looking mansion in a desolate part of town. I tried not to shiver as I took in the creeping ivy, the dark window-panes, the crumbling brick. It screamed horror movie waiting to happen and I couldn't imagine what we'd find inside.

"Is this where the bad vampires live?" I asked. It definitely seemed appropriate.

But Rayne shook her head. "Nope!" she replied with a laugh. "This is Slayer, Inc.'s HQ. I wanted to grab some supplies before we bust into the vampire's den. Also," she added, giving my dress a pointed look. "You need to change. That dress may be amaze-balls, but it's not exactly 'save the day' attire."

"Right," I said, feeling a little disappointed. Not that I minded changing—she was totally right about the outfit being impractical. But I wanted to get this show on the road. After all, who knew what they were doing to Logan in the meantime. He could be suffering. His life could be in danger. While I was distracted by a costume change.

If only I had the ability to do the Superman in a phone booth trick. Though, of course, I wasn't sure there were any phone booths left in the world these days to do it in.

And so I followed Rayne out of the car and into the creepy mansion. Which didn't get any less creepy once we were inside. The place was dark and there didn't seem to be anyone there. Rayne explained it wasn't really the kind of place people lived—more of an office—and at the moment everyone was either off for the night or out on assignment.

We headed for a small office at the far end of the hall. When we got to the door, Rayne reached into her purse and pulled out what appeared to be a lock pick rather than a key. I raised an eyebrow. "I thought you worked here," I said.

She shrugged. "I do. Well, I mean, I did. I guess I'm sort of a consultant nowadays. Since I'm so busy helping Jareth run the Blood Coven and all."

"A consultant without a key?" I queried.

"Dude, do you want to save your boyfriend or not?" she demanded, straightening back up. I sighed.

"He's not really my boyfriend," I started. She gave me a glare. I held up my hands. "Yes, I want to save him," I corrected.

She nodded and went back to her work. A moment later the door sprang open, revealing a small, nondescript office. Well, except for the far wall—which was basically an armory of fancy weapons I'd previously only seen on TV. From shining axes to weird polearms to crazy crossbows straight out of *The Walking Dead*. There were even a few guns—some of them semi-automatic.

I gave a low whistle. "And here I thought you guys just used wooden stakes," I remarked, walking over to the wall.

"Yeah, well, that's sort of the old school way," Rayne admitted. "And honestly, it's still the best. These toys are fun to use, but they complicate things. And they don't fit well in handbags." She walked over to the wall and pulled down a wooden stake I hadn't noticed at first glance. She held it out to me.

I stared down at it, nerves creeping through me. "Oh," I said. "I don't know if I could stake someone..."

"No? Well, we could always go back to the Blood Coven and wait for the *boys* to save the day," Rayne said in a syrupy sweet voice. "If that's what you prefer?"

I sighed and took the stake. "Fine."

"Actually, I think *thank you* was the word you were looking for," she grumbled as she grabbed a few weapons for herself, including that crossbow and another stake. Then she walked over to a wardrobe on the right side wall and pulled it open, rummaging through the rack of clothes inside until she found a long-sleeve black t-shirt and jeans that looked around my size. I took them from her, feeling relived she wasn't going to make me go full-on goth for this mission.

I had just finished changing when we heard the noise. Rayne froze, giving me a worried look.

"Shit," I heard her mutter under her breath. "Busted."

"Busted?" I repeated. "But I thought--"

She put her hand over my mouth. Then, in one fluid motion, she shoved me into the wardrobe. I tried to protest, but she gave me a warning look, then shut the door behind me. A moment later I heard someone step into the room.

"Rayne!" the man's voice said, sounding disapproving. "What the hell are you doing here this late?" He paused, then added, "And in Spider's office, I might add."

"Aww, T-Dogg! It's so good to see you again, too!"

"I told you. Do not call me T-Dogg. Also, I just saw you last night. Why are you here again?"

"Sorry Mr. Teifert. And yeah, it's so strange right? I just can't seem to get enough of this place. In fact, I've been thinking of going back to slaying full time."

"You know the board would never allow you back. Not after last time."

"Oh my God, it was one little house fire! And so not even my fault!"

"House fire? You nearly burned down half the town!"

"Hey! It's not my fault you didn't train me on that cool fire stick thing. I mean Spider got one her first day on the job! And I was stuck with a stupid stake."

"Rayne, you're changing the subject. Why are you here?"

I bit my lower lip, praying she had an answer. One that would satisfy this Teifert guy—whoever he was. The closet was cramped and it didn't have very good airflow. I wasn't sure how long I'd last in here. Not to mention we were wasting precious time. Logan was out there, somewhere. Probably being tortured. We had to get a move on and soon.

My heart thudded in my chest as I thought of Logan. Would

we reach him in time? Would he be okay? Would he be angry that I had come to rescue him when clearly he had done everything in his power to keep me out of this? To keep me safe?

I shook my head. No. He didn't get to make that decision. After all, Jonathan tried to pull that shit with Maisie all the time. That big, bad hero stuff where the guy went all sacrificy on himself to save the girl. But in my books, that never worked out. The girl always saved herself. And, often the guy, too. That was one of the things my fans loved about the books. What I loved about Maisie.

And tonight, I was Maisie. Maybe no longer in her fancy dress, but I was her. And I was going to save Logan. No matter what risk I had to take for myself.

I turned back to the conversation happening outside the wardrobe. Rayne didn't sound like she was doing too well talking her way out of this. And the guy was getting angrier and angrier by the moment.

And, to make matters worse, I was about to sneeze.

I tried to hold it in. I breathed hard through my mouth, pinched my nose with two fingers. But the fibers of one of the coats had entered my nasal passages and the tickling was too severe. A moment later I sneezed. Hard, loud.

"What was that?" Teifert demanded. "You have someone in the closet?"

"Oh for God's sake!" Rayne swore.

The wardrobe door jerked open. An older man stood on the other side, with wild salt and pepper hair and dark eyes. He stared at me, confused for a moment. Then his eyes widened in recognition.

He turned to Rayne. "You've got to be kidding me," he said. "I knew you were a fan! But this--"

"It's not what it looks like!" Rayne blurted out.

"You didn't lock your favorite author in a closet?"

"Well, yeah. I mean, that part. But she came willingly. I swear. She was just...changing clothes when you walked in. And she didn't want you to see her naked."

Teifert glanced at me. I gave him a helpless shrug. "Nice to meet you?" I tried.

He grunted. Rayne gave him a big smile. He raked a hand through his already messed up hair.

"I am too old for this shit," he muttered. Then he turned to Rayne. "The next time I catch you in here, I will bring it up with the board. This is not your office anymore. It belongs to Spider. You have to start respecting that."

Rayne sighed. "Yes, Mr. Teifert," she said. "I was just excited to show my new friend all the cool slayer toys. She's researching, you know? For her next book?"

"Sure," Teifert said. Then he turned to me. "Well, enjoy the rest of your tour." He paused, then added. "And, hey, if you ever need inspiration for a dashing vampire slayer character, well..." He winked. "I'd be happy to--"

"Yeah, yeah. You'll totally be in her next book. And she won't even kill you off. But we've got to go." Rayne grabbed me by the arm and started yanking me toward the door. "By Teif. See you soon!"

And with that, we dashed out of the Slayer Inc. mansion, back to my car. When we got inside, Rayne leaned back in the passenger seat in relief.

"I thought we were totally busted!" she cried.

"Me too." I glanced back at the manor. "Though I left my dress in there."

"I'll get it later," she assured me. "You won't need it where we're going."

"And where are we going?" I questioned, realizing I still had no idea where these big, bad vampires made their home.

Rayne grinned. "Get the motor running and you'll see."

23

I had expected the evil vampires we were tracking down to have an evil mansion somewhere. Maybe even a spooky one like Slayer, Inc. had. Or perhaps, I had thought, they lived underground in some kind of creepy crypt or catacombs like the French vampires had in that *Interview with a Vampire* book.

So imagine my surprise when, as the sun rose over the horizon, Rayne directed me to the gates of a swanky golf course resort instead.

"This is where the evil vampires live?" I asked skeptically.

"I know right?" Rayne rolled her eyes. "They go on and on about wanting to go back to the "old ways" and yet, when it comes right down to it, they don't want to give up all their newfound luxuries. I mean, a true old school vampire would live in a dark, dank, leaky hole somewhere. But not these guys. They want to take over the world—without missing their tee time." She snorted. "Pathetic, if you ask me."

I nodded slowly, not sure what to say. I mean, it did seem a tad inauthentic, but at the same time, I was kind of relieved.

After all, I wasn't sure my nerves could take one of those dark, dank holes.

"So how are we going to break in?"

"Well, that's the best part. It's morning. See the sun is rising? So they're all about to go down underground and sleep. And the golf course will open up to mortals."

"It will?" Now that was shocking.

"Yup! Crazy, right. But vamps need money, too. And without the Consortium's backing, these guys are strapped for cash. So they're forced to find ways to make an income while they try to take over the world."

"By letting humans in."

"Only the richest ones. It's all *very* exclusive. And everything shuts down promptly at six pm. So the workers can clean it before the vampires wake up."

"Wait a second," I said, something suddenly occurring to me. "You're a vampire, right?"

"Uh, yeah."

"So how are you out in the sun?"

"Oh. Right. Well, I'm sort of a mutant. It's a long story. Jareth, too. We can both go out in the sun. Which is a pretty amazing vampire superpower if you ask me."

I silently agreed. Maybe I wouldn't mind being a vampire so much if it wasn't for the sleep all day, party all night thing. I had always been more of a morning person.

"Anyway," Rayne said, back on topic. "I figured we could pose as caterers. No way are they going to believe we are members. We can slip in through the back door and grab aprons in the kitchen."

"And then we search for Logan?"

She nodded. "My guess is he's in some kind of underground area. A basement of some sort. Probably all the vampires are. Look for a door with a big lock. Or maybe an armed guard or two."

I raised an eyebrow. "How are we going to get past an armed guard?"

"Don't worry. I have my methods," Rayne replied. "Now come on. Let's go!"

∽

WE WALKED around the back of the golf club, sure enough finding a service door by the dumpster. We walked in and made our way to the kitchen, grabbing aprons off a hook by the door. A few employees gave us curious looks, but said nothing. I was guessing this place had high turnover with the staff; they probably just assumed we were new.

Finding the secret door, however, proved a lot trickier. The place was huge, with long hallways and a gazillion rooms. And let's just say they didn't exactly advertise their vampire subbasement as one of the amenities.

After about a half hour of searching, Rayne turned to me. "I think we need to split up," she said. "Text me if you find the door and I'll do the same."

I nodded, trying to ignore the creepy feeling in my stomach as I watched her walk away. After all, she had all the weapons, all the experience. What would I do if they caught me?

I shook my head, trying to clear it. There was no use thinking of worst case scenarios. And if Logan was here, well, he needed our help. He had sacrificed himself to save me. I wasn't going to let that be in vain no matter how freaked out I was.

I walked into the next room. A beautiful library with mahogany furniture and built-in bookshelves rising to the ceiling, stuffed with leather-bound tomes. It was the kind of library I always wanted in my home—complete with the little ladder to reach the high shelves. Of course the room was larger than my entire apartment. So that might not work.

Forgetting my mission for a moment, I walked over to the shelves. I pulled out a book at random, pulling it to my nose and breathing in its warm scent. There was just something about the rich smell of old pages that made me calm.

"Hannah? Hannah Miller?"

I whirled around, horrified at the sound of my name. My heart leapt to my throat as a woman rose from one of the armchairs. I hadn't realized anyone was here. And I certainly hadn't realized the president of RAINN, Malory Murphy, was.

For a split second I wondered if I could run out of the room. Maybe she'd think she made a mistake. But no, she was standing between me and the door, a puzzled look on her face. There was no getting out of this.

"Hey!" I cried. "It's so good to see you!"

"It's great to see you, too," she said. Then her brow wrinkled. "Are you...working here?"

"Oh!" I glanced down at my apron, barking out an uneasy laugh. She had to know I made millions with my books. Why would I be here, moonlighting as a caterer? "It's...well, it's a long story."

"I always love your stories," she replied with a smile, relaxing a bit. "How's the new book going anyway?"

I bit my lower lip, my mind racing. "Well, that's an interesting question," I said, suddenly getting an idea. "And exactly why I'm here."

"That sounds mysterious!"

"You ever hear of method acting?" I asked. When she nodded, I went on. "I'm, like, method writing. The plot of my new book involves an exclusive golf club that's actually a front for an evil vampire coven."

She burst out laughing. "I love it!" she cried. Then she

leaned forward conspiratorially. "Most of these guys are quite the bloodsuckers anyway," she said. "Might as well make it literally."

"Actually the true vampires live under the golf club," I explained. "They just rent it out to rich people during the day." I beamed, getting into the swing of things. After all, writers are good liars. That's basically what we do for a living.

Though in this case I was pretty much telling the truth.

She shook her head in amazement. "You are so creative," she said. "I wish I had a mind like yours." She paused, then added, "And it's great to see you getting out, too. I worry about you, you know." She paused, giving me a meaningful look.

I nodded slowly; Malory was one of the only people still in my life who knew what had happened to me that night with Jake. When everyone at school had turned their backs on me, I'd called the RAINN hotline feeling like I had nowhere else to turn. I'd talked to one of their counselors. They'd hooked me up with a local sexual assault survivors group, where Malory worked part-time. Without her I might have never moved forward with my life. My books.

And now...

I looked around the room, amazed, suddenly at where I was. What I was doing. She was right; I never went anywhere. At least not without a major anxiety attack. And now, here I was posing as a caterer in a huge golf club run by vampires, trying to stage a dramatic rescue. The thought was both terrifying and thrilling.

"So, can I be a character?"

I turned back to Malory, cocking my head. "What?"

She grinned wickedly. "In your book, of course! Can I be the one who leads you to the vampire's secret lair?"

"Oh!" I said, taken aback. "Um, yeah? Of course! That would be...great!"

"Hm." She tapped her chin with her finger. "Now if I were a vampire, where would I hide?"

"How about a basement?" I asked, my pulse kicking up in excitement. She was a member here. Maybe she'd have some information that would be useful. "Do you know any basement entrances here?"

"There is a doorway at the back end of the club," she mused. "It's always guarded. At least every time I've ever been here. I figured it was just, like, the club's president's office or something. But..." Her eyes flashed with excitement. "From now on I'm going to assume it's the entrance to a secret vampire lair."

"I love it!" I cried, playing along, even as my insides started dancing with joy. A room in the back with guards? That had to be what we were looking for!

I needed to go find Rayne. Now.

"Well, thank you for your help," I told Malory. "You will make a great character in the book."

She laughed, looking pleased. "Thanks Hannah. And...it's really good to see you out," she added again, placing a warm hand on my arm. "I hope we'll see more of you soon."

I nodded. "You know what? I think I can make that happen."

And with that, I left the library, hurrying down the corridors. I needed to find that door. To find Rayne. To find Logan. And there was no time to waste.

24

I couldn't find Rayne anywhere. But I did eventually find the door. It was just as Malory had described it and armed with two burly guards with firearms strapped to their sides. Oh yes, this had to be it.

But my victory dance was short lived. After all, it wasn't as if these guards were just going to let me just waltz past them to rescue my kidnapped friend. Especially not without making a scene. And the door in question wasn't too far from the main dining room of the golf club where a ton of golfers were milling around, eating breakfast before heading out to the links. The last thing I needed was for one of them to play citizen hero. Or call the police for that matter.

And so I hovered, just around the corner, texting Rayne for the millionth time. But I wasn't sure any of those messages were going through as there was only one bar of cell service on my phone. If only I had asked Malory for the Wi-Fi password...

But it was too late now. Which meant I had to improvise. And if Rayne wasn't around, that meant I had to do it myself. I pursed my lips, thinking hard. Trying to plot this scenario as if it were one of my novels. What would Maisie do in a situation like this? If Jonathan were down there, in desperate need of her help? What could I say to convince the two guards to let me, some random human, into the evil vampire lair they'd been paid to protect? After all, even at the good guy's place—the Blood Coven—I'd had to pretend I was betrothed to Logan to enter past the main doors. And the only other human I'd seen breech the perimeter was...

Oh.

The idea struck me fast and hard. With the force of a ten-ton truck. I thought back to the beautiful black-haired girl who had come knocking on our door. At the time I'd been so jealous of her smug smile and enviable body I hadn't given much thought as to how she got down there. How she was allowed to walk around, unescorted.

But now...

Yes. I could do this. I could totally do this.

Sucking a breath, I turned the corner, swinging my hips as I waltzed up to the two men as if I owned the place.

"Hey guys!" I said, as breezily as I could. As if this was something I did all the time. Just a typical bloody taco Tuesday for a donor chick like me. "How's it hanging?"

The two of them looked down at me, their eyes filled with suspicion. "Who are you?" the first one asked.

"What do you want?" the second one added for good measure.

I giggled. "What do I want?" I repeated. I tapped my chin with my index finger. "Hm. How about a beach house in Cabo? Annual passes to Disney World? Ooh and a bottle of Cristal. I'm a sucker for their rosé."

I paused, then leveled my eyes on them. "But what I need?" I purred. "Is for you to step aside and let me get to work."

The guards frowned. "Sorry," the first one said. "No one's allowed behind these doors. Corporate policy."

I allowed a smile to stretch across my face. "Oh trust me, I'm part of the corporation."

Strutting up to the men, I thrust out my arm and pulled up my sleeve. Sure enough, their eyes widened as they gazed down at the still-fresh bite mark I'd gotten, courtesy of the vampire at the club. The new bite stood out amongst a map of crisscrossed, white scars that could have easily been old vampire bites It was funny; all these years I'd been trying to hide the marks on my arms. Now, they might very well serve to save Logan's life.

"Oh," the second guard sniffed. "You're one of *those*."

"Hey! No need to be all judgey, dude," I shot back, starting to enjoy my new role as sexy blood door. "I mean, not all of us can hope to make a living standing in front of a door all day," I added, giving them a pointed look. "Also, with this I can make my own hours, too. Which is important for a single mom like me."

The guard rolled his eyes. "Sure. Whatever," he said. "It's your life."

"Indeed," I agreed. "So can I go down?" I bit my lower lip, waiting in anticipation. *Please say yes. Please say yes.*

"No."

"No? What do you mean no? They're expecting me!"

"Not for another six hours. It's morning. They're all asleep."

Crap, I hadn't thought about that. Could I suggest one of the vampires had insomnia? That I was like twenty-four-hour room service? But no. They could check that. They might even ask for a name. And then I'd be screwed.

I put a hand to my mouth, leaning toward the men. As if I was ready to spill a secret. "Don't tell anyone," I said in a low voice. "But I like coming early. They have all the cable stations down there. And I am *so* behind on *The Walking Dead*."

The first guard's face lit up. "Oh my God. Then you have no idea they killed off--"

I put my hands over my ears. "No spoilers!" I scolded. Then I removed them. "See? This is why I have to catch up. I've barely been able to get online without accidentally seeing something about last week's episode."

"Oh my God, it was so good! I can't even..." The guard practically bounced with excitement.

I gave him a suspicious look. "Dude, if they killed off Daryl, I am so rioting."

To my delight, the guard stepped away from the door. Then he made a sweeping bow. "Go, watch," he said. "And when you come back up here later, you've got to let me know what you think."

I grinned. "Absolutely."

I was almost through the door when the guard spoke again. "Wait!"

I turned, trying not to look annoyed. Or, you know, scared to death. "What?" I asked.

He reached into his pocket and tossed me a set of keys. "Here," he said. "You'll need these to get into the media room. They keep it locked up during the day."

"Oh. Right. Thank you!" I wrapped my fingers around the keys and shoved them in my pocket. "I'll bring them back up when I'm done."

And with that, I walked right up to the door. They even opened it for me, the perfect gentlemen. A moment later, I was down at the bottom of a set of stairs, inside the vampire's inner sanctum with a set of keys to the kingdom.

I couldn't have planned it better myself.

Pulling out my phone, I sent another text to Rayne, praying she'd get it this time. And that she'd understand why I had to make my move when I could. After all, no way were they going to buy that both of us were donors showing up early to binge watch cable TV, especially with Rayne being a vampire herself.

If she wanted to get down here, she'd have to come up with her own charade.

But my smile soon faded as I took in my new surroundings. It was so dark I had to use my phone's flashlight to look around. The place was massive, likely the entire footprint of the golf club above it and even more opulent. These evil vampires sure knew how to live it up.

But somehow I didn't think Logan would be hanging out in such luxury.

Which meant I had to find him. Now.

crept around the underground lair for the better part of an hour, trying desperately to find Logan. Unlike the Blood Coven, with its cozy bedrooms with soft, comfy beds, this place was more like a prison—with small cells, each containing individual closed coffins. Rayne had said they wanted to go back to the old ways. Guess this was one thing they were bringing back.

Well, that, and sucking people like me dry, that was.

I tiptoed down the dark hallways, trying not to make a sound. I didn't know if vampires in real life were good sleepers, like they always seemed to be in the movies. Or if one of them might be suffering from insomnia and would rise from his coffin at the slightest sound. What would they do if they caught me here? I wondered. Would they kill me instantly? Or keep me around as a captive blood donor for real?

If I was lucky, I would never have to find out. I'd find Logan, rescue him, and get the hell out of here. Never to return.

But where was Logan? I was beginning to get desperate. I'd looked in so many rooms. Tried so many passageways. I'd thought having the keys would help, but every door I unlocked led to a room that was decidedly not a prison. I did wonder, at one point, if maybe they'd stashed Logan in one of the coffins, too. But I wasn't about to start lifting the lids to find out.

Finally, I found a corner I hadn't yet explored. With an imposing door at the end of the hallway, unlike any other in the underground lair. This door had bars on the windows and a not-so-subtle sign that said, "Keep Out. Authorized Vampires Only."

I drew in a breath. This had to be it.

With trembling hands, I reached for my set of keys. Slipped the first one into the lock.

It didn't fit.

I tried the next key. Then the next. And then another and another. But none of them fit. My heart started pounding in my chest, a nagging voice whispering in my ear.

Authorized vampires only. Which meant they wouldn't have given a key to the human guard upstairs.

I leaned against the door, letting out a frustrated groan. I was close. So freaking close. And yet, completely helpless. Was this whole thing just a waste of time from the start? Should we have just waited for Jareth and his diplomatic dealings instead of breaking in?

I turned to the door, kicking it angrily. Logan was in there. I just knew it. And I was completely unable to reach him. Some book heroine I turned out be.

"Move aside, human!"

I startled and almost screamed at the sudden voice. Until I realized it was only Rayne, come up behind me, a big grin on her face.

"There you are!" she cried. "How did you get past the guards?"

I opened my mouth to explain, but she waved me off. "Never mind," she said. "It doesn't matter. What matters is we get to Logan. Before any of these creepy monster vamps wake up."

"I think he's behind this door," I said. "But it's locked. And none of the keys work."

"You have keys, too? Damn. You're good." Rayne gave me an appreciative look. Then she laughed. "But not as good as me."

I watched excitedly as she pulled out her lock picking kit again. The one she had used back at Slayer, Inc.

"Keep watch," she instructed. "I just need a moment."

I glanced down the dark hallway. "Aren't all the vampires asleep?" I asked.

"Yeah, but the guards upstairs aren't. And If I don't do this quick and get back up there, they might start getting suspicious."

"How did you get them to let you pass in the first place?"

"I told them I worked for Vamp Supplies dot com. And I had to make a delivery." She shrugged. "I still had my Slayer, Inc. fake ID. Works like a charm every time."

I nodded, impressed. "Nice."

"Okay. I think I have it. Just need to... Yes!" Rayne crowed as the door creaked open with a loud groan. "Haven't lost my touch!"

I stared down into the darkness. More steps. But unlike the ones we'd already gone down, these ones were made of crumbling concrete. And they looked like they could collapse at any moment.

I turned back to Rayne. "You ready?" I asked.

"No. But you are," she replied.

"What? But I can't--"

"You *have* to," she corrected. "I have to get back up, remember? Or they'll come down here to find me. And if they see this door open..." She trailed off, but I caught her meaning.

I sucked in a breath, trying to squash the fear rising inside of me. "Okay," I said. "I'll go down there and get him out."

"Oh. I'm not sure you'll be able to get him out," Rayne corrected, surprising me.

"What?" I cocked my head. "But isn't that the whole reason we're here?"

"We're *here* to prove they've got him locked up," she explained. "That they're breaking the law. This way the Consortium will have no choice but to order a strike. Then we'll have an entire vampire army at our backs."

"Oh. Right. Okay," I stammered, knowing that this should have been reassuring. A way better plan, actually, than us breaking him out ourselves. But at the same time, it was also disappointing. I wanted to rescue Logan, I realized. Get him out of here now. Not wait for backup.

But that, of course, was completely unrealistic. And at the end of the day I didn't need the glory. I just needed to get Logan out. So I nodded at Rayne.

"Okay," I said. "I'm going down." Then I realized something. "My texts weren't working before. What if they don't work down there either?" After all, the subbasement of a secret evil vampire lair was bound to have even less cell service than the golf club above.

She grabbed my phone. Pressed at the screen. "Wi-Fi password," she said. "I got it off the guard before I came down."

I whistled. "You're good."

"The best," she agreed, flashing me a grin. Then she slapped me on the back. "Good luck," she said before turning to walk back to the stairs, leaving me alone.

I watched her go, adrenaline surging through me all over again.

Good luck indeed. I was going to need it.

26

*T*he good news?

It didn't take me long, once I'd gone down to the subbasement, to find Logan.

The bad?

I barely recognized him when I did.

He was lying on the floor of a prison cell. His once tall, proud body looking crumpled and broken. Hearing my approach, he lifted his head, turning it in my direction. His face, which had always been "vampire pale" was now stark white. His skin, almost translucent. His beautiful blue eyes were bloodshot, rimmed with red. And his whole body was shaking, as if it was an effort for him to move at all.

"Oh Logan," I breathed, stopping in my tracks, trying not to recoil in horror.

At first, he just stared at me. Blankly. As if he couldn't focus his eyes on me to recognize my face. His bewildered expression tore at my heart and it was all I could do not to throw up on the spot as I looked at him, agony tearing through me. I thought back to my tall, proud vampire. The way he moved, the way he commanded a room. Now reduced to a shell of his former self.

I dropped to my knees, forcing the sobs back down my throat. Trying desperately to be brave. To be strong. So he wouldn't have to be. The last thing he needed was to see me fall apart now. I needed to give him hope. A light at the end of the long, dark tunnel he'd evidently been crawling through ever since we parted ways.

"Logan, it's me," I whispered. "It's Hannah."

"Hannah," he rasped. I could see his hard swallow. Caught the flicker of recognition in his eyes. Thank God. "What are you doing here? Did they get you, too?"

I shook my head. "I'm here to rescue you."

He squeezed his eyes shut, as if my words had physically caused him pain. Then he sighed deeply. "You shouldn't have come," he said, so softly I could barely hear him. "You need to leave. Now."

"No way. Not without you."

As I said the words, I realized I meant them. Screw this whole texting a photo and letting vampires save the day plan— though I would do that as well, as backup. But I was not leaving here. Not exiting this room. Not without Logan by my side.

But he didn't seem to appreciate that sentiment. "I'm not leaving," he said in a blank voice. "I made a deal. I came here of my own free will. And I will live up to my word."

"But you'll die down here."

"Then I'll die."

"Please." I scoffed, anger coursing through me now, rejuvenating my resolve. "That's something Jonathan would try to pull. Playing the martyr. The hero. Always trying to sacrifice himself to save the day." I screwed up my face. "Which is all fine and good in my vampire romances. But," I added, meeting his gaze with my own, "Like you said yourself, I don't write *real* vampires. And you, Logan Valcourt, are a *real* vampire. Which means you don't get to make grand sacrifices. You get to survive."

As I punched out the words, I thought I caught a small quivering in Logan's jaw. As if he wanted to laugh, but found it too painful. I pursed my lips, waiting for whatever he would say next. Whatever excuse he would give—I was ready.

"Oh little writer," he said at last. "If only we could have our happily ever after. But this isn't a book. And it isn't going to end well for me. But you..." He turned to look at me again, his beautiful, bloodshot eyes filled with pleading. "You still have a chance. Please, take it. It's the only thing that's keeping me going right now. To know that you will walk away from this. That I haven't taken you down with me."

I drew in a shaky breath. It was the grandest and most beautiful thing anyone had ever said to me. It would have been a great line in a book. One of those lines that gets notated a billion times in people's e-readers.

But again, this was real life, not a story. And it wasn't grand or beautiful or notable. It was messy and complicated. But real.

"Sorry, dude," I shot back, keeping my voice strong. "But it doesn't work like that. I'm a part of this, whether you like it or not. And besides, it's not like they're just going to let me go because they have you." I briefly ran through what happened at the book signing the night before.

"Whatever they promised you, it was a lie," I said when I was finished. "They will kill you and then come after me anyway." I drew in a breath, steeling my nerves. "So wouldn't it be better to stay alive to help protect me from them?"

He groaned, slamming a hand against the cement floor. His knuckles were dry and cracked and started bleeding on contact. I reached in between the bars, taking his hand in mine. Stroking it with gentle fingers. As if I could take the pain away somehow, just by touching him.

Logan sighed deeply. "Don't get me wrong," he said "I would love to protect you. In fact, there's nothing I would want more than to stay by your side forever, keeping you safe. But you don't understand. It's too late. They've taken my blood. I'm too weak. I can't even stand, never mind break out of this place."

My heart fell at the look on his face. He wasn't lying this time. Making any grand gestures. He legitimately couldn't stand up. And there was no way I'd ever be able to carry him, even if I could somehow open his cell.

It was then that I remembered the plan. "Don't worry," I said. "We've got it all worked out. I'm going to take a photo of you and text it to Rayne. She'll send it to Jareth and he'll show it to the Consortium once night falls and everyone wakes up. They'll break you out of here in no time."

Logan gave a weak smile. "That does sound like something out of a book," he admitted. "The Calvary on its way." He squeezed his eyes shut. "But it's not going to work."

"What? Why not?"

"Sweetheart, I don't have time to wait for a rescue. I'm dying. They took too much blood from me. I doubt I have an hour, never mind till nightfall."

Oh God. Oh no.

I bowed my head and closed my eyes, anguish tearing through me now. Everything had seemed as if it was going to work out. To give us that happily ever after, despite the odds. But now... If he was really this close to death... Had so little blood left...

Suddenly, my eyes snapped open. I reached into the cage again, this time turning my hand so the underside of my wrist was exposed. I watched as Logan peered down at the pulsing vein just under my skin. He jerked away, but I shook my arm at him.

"Logan," I commanded. "You have to. You have no choice."

"No." He shook his head. "I would never do that to you."

"You have no choice," I repeated. "If you don't drink from

me, you'll die. You said so yourself. And then they'll come after me." I bit my lower lip, my mind racing. "Trust me, this isn't some charity act. I'm doing it to save my own skin."

"Hannah, you don't know what you're asking," he groaned. "What if I hurt you? I'm so weak. What if I'm not able to stop?"

"Please. You saw me bleeding in the bathroom and you didn't do anything. You're stronger than you give yourself credit for. You can control yourself. I know you can. Just take what you need. Revive your strength. And then we can break out of here. Walk away. We can have that happily ever after in real life that we both want."

He squeezed his eyes shut and I waited for his answer, barely able to breathe in anticipation of what he would say. *Please,* I begged silently. *Please don't be stubborn.*

Finally, he turned to me. Blood tears dripped down his cheeks, splashing onto my hand. For a moment, he just looked at me. An agonized look that nearly broke my heart. Then, he leaned down, taking my wrist in his hand and bringing it to his mouth. For a moment he just hovered there and I held my breath, anticipation buzzing through me. I was terrified. But I was also a little excited. This was it. The moment I had written about a thousand times, now about to happen to me.

And then his mouth closed over my wrist. His fangs sinking into my flesh. I gritted my teeth, waiting for the pain, like when the vampire in the alleyway bit me. But it never came. Instead, there was a flash of unexpected pleasure flooding my insides until I almost cried out with joy.

Suddenly it was as if we had become one person, the floodgates opening and emotions and memories flooding through me. I could feel Logan as I could feel myself—all his anguish, his fury rushing through me like a raging river, euphoric at finally being freed.

But at the same time I felt something else, too. Something

beyond anger and fury. Something...sweeter. Something that seemed a little bit scared. Afraid to let go and trust what was happening here.

He'd been hurt, I realized suddenly. Badly. The face of a woman swirled through my mind. Perhaps his maker? The one who turned him into the creature he was today? I had always assumed he liked being a vampire—he was so arrogant about the whole thing. But now...

Now I wasn't so sure.

My thoughts and emotions began to blur into one another then and it became suddenly difficult to keep them straight. Colors flashed before my eyes. Warmth floated through my body.

I wanted to sleep. To sleep forever would be—

Logan broke away, startling me back to the present. It was as if someone had dumped a bucket of ice cold water over my head and I barely managed not to scream in protest. The warmth fled. The colors faded. And I was left with an aching wrist and a terrible headache. And a weakness that was so overpowering that now it was I who could barely stand.

"I'm sorry," I could hear Logan whisper. "I tried to stop. I tried--"

I held up my hand to stop him. "I'm fine," I assured him, even though I didn't know if that was true. I pulled my knees to my chest, wondering for a moment where we were. My head was pounding and it was still hard to pull thoughts together. To think at all.

I could feel Logan's eyes on me. Burning with self-loathing. "I need to get out of here," he said. "Let me work on the lock."

I nodded absently, thinking about what I had learned about him during our blood bond. The secret I now knew. The hatred he felt for his own kind. The hatred he felt for himself and what he'd become. No wonder he was so angry about my books. The glamorization of being a vampire. Creatures living beautiful, immortal lives with riches beyond belief and true loves to keep them warm. Logan didn't have a true love. And the emptiness I felt inside of him had been cavernous.

God, I was tired. I lay down on the floor, figuring I could just rest my eyes for one minute...

"Hang in there, sweetheart," I heard him say. "I've almost got it..."

"I don't think so."

I jerked my head at the unfamiliar voice, suddenly wide awake. A tall, broad-shouldered man stood in the doorway, silhouetted by the light behind him.

No, my mind corrected. *Not a man.*

A vampire.

27

*I*t didn't take long for the vampire to assess the situation. For him to make his move. One moment he was at the door. The next he was on top of me, grabbing me by the shoulders, digging his filthy nails into my flesh. He jerked me to my feet, staring down at me with greedy eyes.

"Let her go!" Logan growled. "Or I'll rip your head off."

The vampire ignored him, shoving me against the wall. My back hit hard and I wondered wildly if he'd broken it. I collapsed to the ground, pain searing through me. I wanted to get up, to fight back. But I was so weak from giving so much of my blood. Which must have been how he found us here in the first place. The scent of my blood making him rise from his coffin early. Like coffee to a sleepy human.

Logan shoved his entire weight at the cell door, desperate to save me. He already looked better, I noticed bleakly. His face not so pale. His body no longer shrunken from dehydration. He slammed himself at the door again and it groaned loudly—but stuck fast.

The vampire turned to Logan, giving him a derisive look.

"Just like a Consortium Member," he spit out, clicking his tongue in disapproval. "Always falling in love with their dinner."

"Just let her go," Logan said again. "We had a deal."

"A deal that you are clearly breaking," the vampire replied, observing him with cool eyes. "You're trying to escape."

"I'm trying to get *her* out of here."

"She has two feet. Surely she's capable of walking out herself." The vampire glanced over at me with a small smirk. "Or, at least, crawling like the worm that she is."

"I won't leave without Logan," I croaked, surprised at how difficult it was to speak.

"How adorable," the vampire sniffed. "The cattle in love with the butcher." He walked over to me. "Stupid girl. You should already be dead for what you did. I know you had a part in Cedric's death."

"Cedric tried to kill me."

"So? Do you think your life has any value to me? You're nothing but a tiny appetizer. Once we get Pyrus back in charge, you humans will learn your proper place in this world."

"You're not getting Pyrus out," Logan growled. "Lord Magnus and the Consortium will never allow him to walk free."

The vampire shrugged. "Maybe not. But that doesn't mean we won't prevail in the end. We tried to work through the courts. To plead our case using your laws. But you went and killed our witness. So now we are forced to take another tact."

"And what might that be?"

"Please. You think I would tell you? This isn't a movie with the bad guy giving away his evil scheme. Just know this, Logan Valcourt. You dealt us a blow by murdering Cedric, yes. But we are not one vampire. We are legion. And we will come for you all." He smiled. "Well, for your precious Blood Coven anyway. You'll, of course, already be dead."

Logan roared with rage, trying to break the cage again. But it held fast. He gave me a heartbreaking look. "Please," he begged. "Just go."

"No," I said, tears streaming down my cheeks. "I won't leave you."

"So sweet," the vampire purred. "I actually believe you care about her." He grabbed me again, lifting me up. This time into the air so my feet dangled. I kicked at him, but he only laughed. "They're so fragile," he observed. "Yet so feisty. I love it."

"Let her go!" Logan cried. "I'll do what you say. I'll do anything. Just don't--"

But his cries went unanswered. The vampire shoved me back against the wall. He turned and winked at Logan. "Thanks for leaving me the last drops," he said.

Then he leaned forward, piercing my neck with his fangs.

screamed in agony as the vampire's teeth drove into me, hard and fast and cruel. The exact same action that Logan had taken only moments before, yet so much different in intention and feeling. What had once caused pleasure and warmth with Logan, now only brought on unbearable pain and suffering as the vampire tore at my skin. Siphoning my blood. His hand clamped against my neck, making it difficult to breathe.

I struggled wildly, arms and legs flailing, landing weak hits to his stomach and head. But he didn't even acknowledge my pathetic attempts to regain control. And soon I was forced to stop anyway—no strength to continue. My body went limp. Stars danced across my vision. The blackness began to roll in like a thick fog.

In the end, it was all I could do to open my eyes. To turn my head and look at Logan, who was still trying to break free from his cell. He caught my gaze, returning a devastated look that shattered my heart into a million pieces.

If I had to die, I'd die looking at him. That would be something at least. In fact, that would be everything.

Because I *was* dying, I realized vaguely. There was no getting out of that. The vampire author would be drained dry by a vampire. It was almost a poetic way to go.

Yet, at the same time, pathetic, right? I mean, if this were a book this would never happen. I'd come up with some creative way to overpower him. To save myself and Logan, too.

But, it seemed, reality was a lot harder than fiction. I was weak. The vampire was strong. And I was no Buffy. No chosen girl with special powers and a stake that—

Holy shit. I had a stake!

With all that had happened, I had completely forgotten Rayne handing over that chunk of wood back at Slayer, Inc. HQ. I'd stuck it in my bag and had totally forgotten it was there. Was it still there? I tried to glance over at my discarded bag in the corner of the room. Yes. I could see it, peeking out from the side pocket. If only I could get to it somehow…

My head spun. My stomach wrenched. Which suddenly gave me an idea. I reached up with a shaky hand, sticking a finger down my throat.

Forcing myself to throw up on the vampire.

"What the hell?" he cried, breaking away as hot yellow vomit sprayed at his face. "Did you just fucking puke on me?"

I didn't answer. Instead, I dropped to the floor, rolling across it until I reached my bag. I could hear him lunging after me, but I didn't pause. Instead, I grabbed the stake and whirled around. Just in time for him to tackle me. I shoved the stake upward with all my remaining strength.

I didn't miss.

He started to scream. But it didn't last long. His body exploded into a cloud of dust. For a moment it seemed to hover above me. Then it dropped down on me like a blanket of dirt. I coughed as vampire soot filled my mouth.

"Ew!" I sputtered, rolling over, trying not to throw up again. "So gross!"

"Hannah!" I could hear Logan cry.

And then he was there. Out of his cage. By my side. Grabbing me into his arms, he pulled me to him with a fierceness that could have broken my bones. I cried out in protest and he seemed to realize what he was doing, loosening his hold, just a bit. I collapsed against him, desperate to absorb his strength.

"Nice of you to join me," I managed to say with a weak smile.

"Oh sweetheart," he murmured, stroking my hair. "That was so amazing. I thought---I thought..."

"Hm. Maybe you don't know humans as well as you thought you did," I managed to tease. But it took effort. I was so weak. So dizzy. So sick.

Logan pulled me away from him, studying me with worried eyes. "You've lost too much blood," he said, his voice filled with fear. "That bastard. I would rip him apart--limb from limb." He gave me a wry smile. "If only you hadn't already done the job."

I smiled weakly, loving the fury and indignation in his voice. I reached up with a trembling hand, brushing his cheek with my fingers. Wanting to feel him one more time.

Because I was pretty sure this was it. This was the end of my story.

"I'm so cold," I whispered. "So, so cold."

He let out a horrible moan. "No!" he cried. "I can't lose you. Not now. Not after everything. But..." he trailed off, looking miserable. Torn.

My eyes widened, suddenly realizing what he was thinking. What part of the story we now found ourselves in. The part that came in almost every vampire novel. The decision every vampire and human got to make.

Our blood bond might have been broken, but I could still feel Logan's agony raging through him like wildfire. His doubt, his hesitation, his fear. He wanted nothing more than to save my life and he knew only one way to do it. But he wasn't sure if he should. If he could. To force me into the life he hated so much. To make me a monster like him.

But, in the end, it wasn't his choice to make. It was my life, after all.

I drew in a shaky breath. "Let me drink from you," I managed to say, my whole body still trembling. And not with fear this time. Rather hunger. My desire to go on burning through me like a fever. Suddenly I knew, no matter what, I couldn't let it end like this. I'd finally found something worth living for. But I would have to die to get it.

I didn't necessarily want to become a vampire. But if that was my only choice I was going to grab onto it with both hands. After all, how could I just give up? Let that bastard and his band of vampire vigilantes win? This wasn't nearly over. Sure, we'd killed one of them—well, two of them. But like he'd said, they were legion. And as long as their fearless leader Pyrus was still alive, the world was not safe. For vampires...or humans.

Also, there was Logan. My Logan.

I lifted my eyes. "Please," I said. "Don't make me beg."

He raked a hand through his hair, his eyes filled with agony. "You don't know what you're asking."

"Of course I do. I'm not an idiot."

"This isn't like a novel."

"I think I know the difference between fact and fiction."

"I'd be cursing you for eternity. You'd never see the sun again."

"The sun is overrated."

"You'd never get to eat food. You'd never get to have a baby."

I swallowed hard. "But I'd have you," I whispered.

Something inside of him seemed to break. Blood tears

flowed from his eyes. He drew in a breath. "Are you absolutely sure?" he whispered.

"I'm sure."

With a choking sob, he pulled up his sleeve. His fangs extended. He put his mouth to his arm, ripping open his skin at the wrist. Then he pressed it against my mouth.

And I drank deeply.

The blood flowed, thick and sweet and syrupy into me. I moaned in pleasure, lapping up each and every drop and gulping it down. As I did, I opened my mind up to him. Not holding anything back. I had seen his dark secrets. His pain. Now it was time to share my own. All the horrors of that rape. All the years of being alone, scared to share my life with anyone again. I gave it all to him without holding back. Every humiliation, every embarrassing cut I'd made behind closed doors, terrified someone would find out. But with Logan, I had nothing to hide. He accepted me for who I was. And I was better because of it.

And soon, I would be better still.

Finally, he pulled his arm away. I cried out for a moment in protest, wanting more. So much more. A smile played at the corner of his lips. He pressed a finger to my mouth. "Greedy girl," he teased. "They'll be time for more later. But first, how about we get out of the bad guy golf club before anyone else wakes up?"

I nodded, feeling the strength already rising within me. "Now that's the best idea I've heard all day."

29

*W*e waited until moments before sunset before making our way up out of the basement and into the main golf club. I wasn't sure what explanation we would give the guards on our way back up, but it turned out Rayne had already thought of that. They were lying on the ground when we stepped through the door, sleeping like babies, half-drunk glasses of some kind of liquid in their hands.

When Rayne saw me, she rushed toward me, arms outstretched. "Oh thank God!" she cried, throwing herself into an enthusiastic hug between us. "When you didn't text me, I thought the worst! I was trying to get down again, but they wouldn't let me. So I had to improvise with a little Slayer Inc. sleeping potion." She grinned wickedly. "Just don't tell Teifert I stole his stash. He's still sore about the time I used it to draw a mustache on his face with permanent Sharpie while he slept."

I rolled my eyes. "Your secret is safe with me."

"Anyway! I'm so glad you got him out. Logan, you are an idiot. Don't do that to yourself again."

He smiled at her. "That I can promise."

Rayne turned from him to me. "And you. You are covered in

vampire dust. Did you get to put that stake I gave you to good use?"

"I did actually," I said, grinning from ear to ear. "Guess it's not such a lame weapon after all."

"Oh it's totally lame," she corrected. "But sometimes lame does the trick." Then her eyes narrowed. "Wait a second," she said. "Something's different about you."

I felt my cheeks heat. "Uh, yeah. We ran into a little trouble and--"

"OH MY GOD YOU'RE A VAMPIRE!" Rayne screeched. She jumped up and down, crowing loudly. "I can't believe it! This is the best thing ever!"

"Calm down," Logan scolded. But he was smiling as he said it.

"And you said you'd never turn anyone," Rayne accused, turning to him. "What happened to the joy of solitude and all that dumb stuff you used to go on about?"

He shrugged sheepishly. "Sometimes life surprises you."

"Best surprise ever," Rayne declared. "I mean, here I was, so worried you'd die down there before you got to Jade's story. But now! Now you're immortal! Which means the Maisie and Jonathan series can go on forever and ever!" Her eyes flashed with excitement. "I bet you'll be able to write faster now, too. And maybe I could be your beta reader? So I could read the books before anyone else?"

I laughed, holding up my hand. "Can I just have a day or two getting used to being an immortal creature of the night before you put me back to work?"

Rayne giggled. "Oh. Yeah. Sure. Of course. It's actually kind of a rough transition, if you want to know the truth. But if you need any help--"

"We'll be fine, Rayne," Logan said, cutting her off in a firm voice.

"Of course you will! You'll be more than fine! You're going to be a fantastic couple. Just like me and Jareth. Together forever." Rayne mock swooned while I resisted the urge to blush all over again.

Fantastic couple. So were we a couple now? I mean, sure, we were bonded by blood, but did that make us...what was it they called it? Blood mates? I took a shy glance over at Logan. He looked a little nervous, too. Not surprising. This was a big step for him as well. And certainly not something he'd been planning.

I reached out and took his hand. Then I squeezed it, giving him a small smile. He smiled back, squeezing my hand in return. My stomach warmed. Maybe this could work.

No. No maybe about it. This *would* work.

"Rayne, I need you to go to Jareth," Logan said, getting back to business. "Tell him everything that happened here. We now have proof that these renegades are trying to overthrow the Consortium. With our testimonies, I imagine we can at least keep Pyrus locked up. If not put a few of the others in prison with him." He gave her the details of what we learned. She listened carefully, then nodded.

"All right," she said. "I'll go tell him. He's going to be pissed we did this on our own. But hey, he's usually pissed at me about something or other anyway, so no big deal." She laughed, then turned serious. "What are you guys going to do?"

Logan turned and looked at me. "I thought we'd lay low for a bit," he said. "Get Hannah adjusted to her new life."

Rayne winked at him. "Adjusted, huh? Is that what the kids are calling it these days?" she teased. Then she slapped me on the back. "Just don't adjust too long. I'm expecting chapters of the new book. And I'm not very patient."

"I'll send some over tomorrow," I promised her. "You deserve that at least, after all your help. Obviously I couldn't have done this without you."

"Obviously," she said. But she looked pleased.

Logan turned to me. "Are you ready?" he asked.

I slipped my hand into his. "Let's go home."

30

I'd love to tell you that the rest of that night was easy. Or that I was completely adjusted to my new life as a vampire by the time the sun rose in the sky the next day. But reality was a lot crueler than a vampire novel. And instead of a romantic night, I spent half the time in the bathroom, puking my guts out while my body raged with fever. It was like the worst flu I ever had times a thousand. Which wasn't surprising, I supposed, since technically I was dying. At least the human part of me was.

But after the death came the rebirth. And that made it all worth it in the end.

It was funny in a way. All my career people had asked me: would I choose to become a vampire if I had the chance? And I would always answer no. But now that it was actually happening, I didn't mind it as much as I thought I would. In fact, it was sort of like being given a brand new life. Still me, only better. I could shed the skin of my former self. All my anxiety, my inhibitions, all the guilt and fear and anger from what had happened in my past. All of that fell away as my vampirism began to take hold. Instead of a dark, lonely life, there was nothing but hope and possibility now. No one could hurt me. I didn't need to hide away.

Well, that wasn't technically true. I mean I still had to stay inside during the day—that was going to be quite a bummer at first. And I'd never again get to taste the awesome of pepperoni pizza or chocolate ice cream. Logan told me he'd set me up with a blood donor, but if I wanted to try synthetic blood at first, just until I was used to it, that would be okay, too. We would make it work.

And *we* would make us work, too. That was something I was sure about. I may not have known Logan long, but I knew him as well as I knew myself. Now that we'd bonded, shared our blood, shared our sorrows and pain. I knew he would never hurt me, never leave me and would do everything possible to keep me safe. Not that I hadn't done a knock up job of saving myself, thank you very much. But sometimes it was nice to have backup.

Especially sexy, yummy broad-shouldered, six-pack abs backup like Logan.

WE SPENT the next day sleeping, of course, and when night fell I was starting to feel a bit better. Logan gave me a blood cocktail which was actually pretty delicious (I drank it out of a martini glass) and we settled into the living room of his home to watch a movie.

Yes, real vampires watched movies. There was a lot I was learning.

Of course we barely paid attention to the actual film. Because real life was suddenly becoming a lot more interesting than anything on TV. And soon I found myself once again curling my new, powerful body into Logan's strong frame. Wrapping my arms around his neck and pulling him toward me. He looked down at me, adoration swirling in his beautiful blue eyes.

"Again?" he teased. "Why, Miss Miller, you have developed quite the appetite."

I blushed. "Gotta make up for lost time."

"And here we are. With all the time in the world."

He reached out, taking my jaw in his hand and tilting my head until my lips were lined up with his. Then he leaned forward, pressing his mouth against mine. Hard, fast, unyielding. As if I were some gourmet dessert and he hadn't eaten in years.

I smiled against his mouth, kissing him back in return. The sensations flowed through me igniting every nerve. But there was no doubt or fear left inside. What Jake had stolen from me all those years ago? I'd gotten it back, tenfold. And I would never let anyone hurt me again. Or take something away from me that was so pure and good and make it into something evil.

From now on I was in charge of me. And right now this "me" wanted a piece of Logan.

I rolled over, straddling him with my thighs, my lips never leaving his. He groaned in pleasure, his hands gripping my hips, then rising up to graze my stomach. Electricity shot through me and soon I was burning all over again from his touch.

Fun fact: vampires felt things a thousand times more strongly than people did. Meaning it was almost too much, while at the same time not nearly enough.

"I want you," I whispered in his ear, daring myself to nibble the lobe. He rocked against me and I could feel his desire rising to meet my own. He wanted me too. That was for sure.

And there was nothing left in our way.

He grabbed the remote. Turned off the film. Laid me down on the couch and pulled down my pants. I sucked in a breath, for one split second feeling exposed and scared all over again.

But then he tilted my head back up, so I was forced to meet his eyes. His beautiful, kind eyes that held no deception. I could trust him. He would never hurt me.

The connection that flowed between us was both powerful and sweet at the same time. And after, he collapsed on top of me, his breathing hard and heavy, I rolled over, cradling my head in his nook. He reached up, stroking my hair.

"Are you okay?" he asked.

"I'm perfect," I said with a happy sigh. "In fact, I've never been better."

Then something occurred to me. And I laughed.

He propped himself up on his elbow, staring down at me. "What?" he asked.

"Nothing," I said. "It's just..." I shook my head, amusement dancing through me. "When you walked into that bookstore during my signing. When you told me I didn't know anything about vampires—or men for that matter?"

He groaned, dropping back down to the couch. "You have to bring that up again, now?" he asked.

I playfully poked him in the stomach. "You were right," I told him. "I didn't know. I thought I did. But I had no freaking clue. But now... I'm beginning to get an idea."

He smiled, revealing his fangs. Fangs which had once scared me, but now looked pretty damn sexy as part of his smile. I wondered, suddenly, if vampires ever drank from one another just for fun.

There was a lot I still didn't know. But I was eager to find out.

"So does this mean I win the bet?" he asked throatily.

I broke out laughing. "I forgot we even made one. What was it again?"

"That I would convince you, beyond a shadow of a doubt, that vampires existed."

"Well, mission accomplished. I guess you win. What was your prize again?"

"That you stay with me for a weekend."

"I think I can do better than that," I said with a grin. "How about an immortal lifetime?"

"I could live with that."

We kissed again, though it was actually kind of difficult, as we were both smiling so much. And then the kiss deepened and I could feel him becoming aroused again. One more thing to add to my vampire notes: they had amazing stamina.

Good thing I'd now be able to keep up.

"Hannah," he whispered. "I can't even begin to tell you--"

But he never finished. Because suddenly there was a knock at the door.

We looked at one another. My non-beating heart was in my throat. Who could that be? Was it just one of the Blood Coven members, coming to check on us? Or...

Logan rose to his feet and grabbed his jeans, slipping them over his hips and zipping them closed. He turned to me, his eyes wide and serious. Then he nodded his head toward the closet at the far end of the room.

At first I wanted to protest, but I realized it would do no good. He wasn't going to open the door with me standing there —afraid of putting me at risk. I was still pretty weak from my transition, after all. Until I gained strength, I had to be content to still act like a human.

And so I slunk into the closet, pulling the door closed behind me. Deciding that if there was any trouble, I would jump out to help.

I watched from the sliver in the door crack as Logan went to the front door. He looked through the peephole and I saw his face pale. I swallowed hard. Oh God. What was on the other side? One of those horrible vigilante vampires, out for blood? A member of Slayer, Inc. with a new contract to kill?

As I watched, Logan pulled the door open wide, revealing a woman standing behind it. A small, thin woman dressed all in black. Breathtakingly beautiful with pale skin, huge red lips and dark, mysterious eyes.

Another vampire, I realized. But who?

"Oh my God." Logan exclaimed, his voice hoarse and filled with dread. Whoever this vampire was, she was clearly not someone he'd expected to see. "You're...I thought you were... Oh my God."

The woman didn't seem to notice. She stepped into the house, walking right up to him. Then, to my horror she wrapped her arms around him, dragging him to her until their bodies were flush against one another.

"Come now, baby," she purred. "Is that any way to greet your Maker?"

~~ **To be continued** ~~

THE TALES FROM THE BLOOD COVEN CONTINUE WITH...

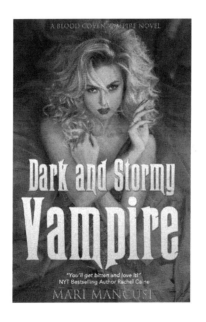

Hannah and Logan's adventures continue with DARK AND STORMY VAMPIRE - the second book in the Tales from the Blood Coven series, coming this February.

In the meantime, please turn the page to learn about the books that started it all — the original eight book Blood Coven Vampire series, starring Rayne MacDonald and her twin sister Sunny.

*T*wo sisters—as different as the sun and the rain. For one, getting into the Blood Coven is to die for. But for the other, getting out could be lethal.

When Sunny MacDonald doesn't know what to expect when she's dragged to Club Fang by her twin sister Rayne. But when the devastatingly handsome Magnus mistakes her for her goth-loving twin and bites her on the neck, she realizes his fangs are all too real...and all too deadly.

Now Sunny and Magnus find themselves in a race against time to find a way to reverse the bite before Sunny becomes a vampire forever. Something she definitely shouldn't want—even if it does mean spending eternity with a certain boy who bites...

"If you liked Buffy and Angel, you will love this." — Eternal Night

"Delightful, surprising, and engaging. You'll get bitten and love it." — Rachel Caine, NYT Bestselling Author of the Morganville Vampire series

FIND IT AT BOOKS2READ.COM/MARIMANCUSI.

The Blood Coven Vampires Reading List
Boys that Bite
Stake That
Girls that Growl
Bad Blood
Night School
Blood Ties
Soul Bound
Blood Forever

Tales from the Blood Coven
Once Upon a Vampire
Dark and Stormy Vampire (February 2018)

Made in the USA
Monee, IL
12 May 2020

30816160R00114